SUGAR CREEK GANG
THE
KILLER CAT

SUGAR CREEK GANG
THE
KILLER CAT

Original title:
We Killed a Wildcat at Sugar Creek

Paul Hutchens

MOODY PRESS • CHICAGO

We Killed a Wildcat at Sugar Creek
Copyright ©, 1958, by
Paul Hutchens
Moody Press Edition 1966

Printed in the United States of America

1

THE FIRST TIME anybody around Sugar Creek knew for sure there was a bloodthirsty, savage-tempered wildcat in the territory was when one of them sneaked into Harm Groenwald's pasture and killed three of his prize lambs.

I never will forget the hair-raising chills that ran up and down my spine the morning I first heard about it. Since Harm Groenwald's pasture was the first field next to our farm on the South, that great big twenty-eight-toothed, fierce-fighting killer had been close enough to us to have killed some of our *own* livestock—close enough to scare our family half to death if we had known about it.

We had just finished breakfast at our house when we got the news. It had been one of the most peaceful breakfasts we had had in a long time, with Charlotte Ann, my mischievous-minded, usually-hard-to-manage baby sister, being especially well behaved, not fussing nor whining but behaving like most babies don't in the morning.

My grayish-brown-haired mother was sipping her coffee quietly and had a very contented look on her face as we all waited for my bushy-eye-browed, reddish-brown-mustached father to finish reading the Bible story he had just started.

I didn't have any idea as I listened that part of what he was reading was going to get mixed up in the excitement of a wildcat hunt before the summer would pass.

The short Bible story was about a grown-up boy named Jacob who had had a quarrel with his brother, Esau, and to save his life had left home to go to another country where his mother used to live.

The first night of the long journey had to be spent in a very rocky territory with steep cliffs and outcroppings and different shaped boulders piled on each other. It made me think of the rocky hills above Old Man Paddler's cabin. In fact, the hills in that part of Sugar Creek territory were not far from the haunted house we all knew about, and they were the best place in the world for wildcats to live and hunt and raise their families. Of course, I didn't think of that while Mom was sipping her coffee, and Charlotte Ann was playing with her cute, pink, bare toes and Dad was reading along in his deep, gruff voice.

Anyway, while Jacob slept that night outdoors

—using a stone for a pillow—he had a dream about a ladder or stairway leading all the way up to heaven. In the dream he saw angels going up and down the ladder.

In a minute Dad would finish reading and we'd have what Mom calls a Quaker prayer meeting. That means we'd all be quiet a minute and each one would think his own prayer to God just before Dad or Mom or maybe I would pray with actual words—and our day would be started right.

Then is when, all of a startling sudden, the phone started ringing in our front room.

I listened to see whether it was going to ring our ring or somebody else's. I knew all the gang's numbers by heart: two longs and a short for Little Jim, two shorts and a long for Poetry, three shorts for Circus, two shorts for Big Jim, four shorts for Dragonfly, and ours was one long and one short.

Different other neighbors had different other numbers.

All anybody on our seven-phone party line had to do if he wanted to talk to any other family on the line was to go to the phone, lift the receiver, and ring whatever number he wanted.

Of course, everybody on the party line could hear the phone ring in their own house at the same time and would know who was *being called* but *not* who was *calling*—unless they lifted their own receiver and did what is called "eavesdropping." Nobody was supposed to do that, but different people sometimes did and made different people mad at each other.

There was also a very special ring which was hardly ever used. It was called an "emergency ring," and nobody was supposed to ring it unless there was an actual emergency, such as an accident or a death in the family or somebody's cow had run away and couldn't be found. That emergency ring was two extra long longs and two very short shorts.

Well, our heads were all bowed at our breakfast table, and I was in my imagination up in the hills not far from the haunted house lying on a stone pillow watching angels moving up and down the golden stairway sort of like people riding up and down on an escalator in a city department store. And *that* is when I heard the jangling of the phone in our living room. My mind was jarred all the way back to our kitchen table and I was hearing the extra-long long, followed by another just-as-long long and then two short, sharp shorts.

"*Emergency!*" Mom in her chair beside Charlotte Ann's high chair exclaimed, jumping like a scared rabbit that had been shot at and missed. A startled look came over her face and she was out of her chair in a flurry of a hurry, accidentally knocking her chair over to get across the kitchen floor as fast as she could into the living room and to the phone to answer it.

All that excitement brought Charlotte Ann to baby-style life. Her arms flew out and up in several directions, she knocked over her blue mug of white milk which spilled over the edge of her chair tray and splashed onto the floor. Mixy, our black and white tame house cat, came to excitement from her box of straw by the kitchen stove and started in lapping up as much of the spilled milk as she could before anybody in the family could mop it up and it'd be wasted.

In the living room Mom's voice gasped out, "What! A wildcat! Who said so! How do you know!"

I was out of my chair even faster than Mom had gotten out of hers. I stood beside her at the phone straining my ears to see if I could hear whosever voice was on the other end of the line, but I couldn't. That is, I couldn't hear any *one* voice. Instead, because Mom had her receiver about an inch from her ear, I heard a jumble of what sounded like a dozen women's voices, with everybody talking to everybody and almost nobody listening to anybody.

I tell you there was a lot of excitement around our house after Mom hung up and explained what

the emergency really was. It was Harm Groenwald's fast-talking wife who had rung the emergency number. They'd had three of their prize
lambs killed last night. Their carcasses had been
torn in the same way that two of their other lambs
had been eaten into a year ago.

"This time I'm going to find out what killed
them!" Harm told his wife. "I'm going to call
Chuck Hammer."

Chuck, the Sugar Creek veterinarian, had hurried out from town to have a look at the dead
lambs. He used to live out West and had seen kills
like that before. He turned the bodies over a few
times and said grimly, "We've got either a mountain lion or a monster wildcat on our hands. They
both kill the same way. See here?"

He showed Harm what he meant. "They always
crush the neck bones in front of the shoulders, then
tear into the carcass *behind* the shoulders and eat
out first the heart and liver."

"But whoever heard of a mountain lion or a
wildcat around here?" Harm objected. "They don't
live in this part of the country!"

"*One* does," Chuck said—"and he's a *big* one!
Huge!"

A few jiffies later they found its tracks in a muddy place, and Chuck called out "Wildcat! I'd say
thirty-five pounds, anyway. Maybe forty-five!"

Harm Groenwald's fast-talking, high-pitched-voiced wife had told all that to all the people who had answered the emergency ring—told it in less than a minute and a half. It took Mom almost three minutes to tell it to Dad and me.

Dad quick got on the phone then and asked the vet who was still at Groenwald's house to stop at our farm on the way back to town. Addie, our old red mother hog, had given us a litter of six pigs last night, and Dad thought Chuck ought to look her over and maybe suggest a better diet for her so her babies would grow stronger fast, twelve different ways.

I helped Mom clean up Charlotte Ann's spilled milk and finished just in time to go out to the hog lot where Dad and Chuck were talking about the monster of a wildcat and also where Chuck was giving Addie a physical checkup.

"She's all right," Chuck told Dad. "She's given you six of the healthiest pigs I've ever seen. Not a runt in the litter."

Poetry, my almost best friend, had heard the emergency ring and was on his way over to our house to talk it over with me. He'd hitched a ride with Chuck, so he was there too. That was one reason why I didn't *quite* finish helping Mom clean

11

up the kitchen. I needed to get out where all the excitement was.

Standing by Addie's gate, Poetry started in singsonging a little ditty he'd learned somewhere:

"Six little pigs in the straw with their mother,
Bright eyes, curly tails, tumbling on each other;
   Bring them apples from the orchard trees,
And hear those piggies say, 'Please, please, please.'"

It was a cute little rhyme and I told Poetry so that started him off singsonging it again.

Right that minute there was a glad feeling singsonging itself in my mind. In fact there had been ever since Harm Groenwald's wife had told Mom and Mom had told Dad and me that it was a wildcat that had killed Harm's last year's *two* lambs, as well as this year's *three*. It had been a wildcat and not a dog that had done it.

I reckon you know *why* I was glad if you've read the story *10,000 Minutes at Sugar Creek*. I never will forget those 10,000 minutes—which is how many minutes it took for the week to pass. Wally, my city cousin, had spent the whole 10,000 minutes at our farm. And Alexander the Coppersmith, his non-sensical, ill-mannered, city-bred dog, had been with him. The most uncontrollable dog there ever was, I reckon.

Anyway, the night Harm Groenwald's two

12

lambs had been killed was the same night Wally's nervous mongrel had unleashed himself, and it had been *my* fault for his collar being too loose. My fault, I had thought again and again, that two innocent lambs had been killed!

One reason I hadn't told anybody was 'cause if they ever proved it was Wally's dog that had done it, Alexander'd have to be shot, and I'd be to blame for *his* death too. It'd be a shame for a city dog that didn't know any better to have to lose his life.

So I'd put off telling anybody, but I shouldn't have. I should have told what Alexander did that same summer before Wally took his dog home to Memory City with him.

And now I'd never have to! Feeling glad in my heart toward God for making everything work out the way it had, and because I was in the habit of talking outloud to Him anytime I felt like it, I all of a sudden, without knowing I was going to do it, said, "Thanks! Thanks a lot!"

Poetry, not knowing what I'd been thinking, answered with his squawky duck-like voice, "I'm glad you like it. I'll sing it again." And he was off in another half-bass singsong about the six little pigs in the straw with their mother.

We were all interrupted then by the sound of dogs' voices coming from the direction of Harm Groenwald's pasture. I'd heard those same long-toned, long-voiced hounds before. My mind's eye told me it was Jay and Bawler, Circus' father's big coon hounds. They were on the trail of the wild-cat. Already Harm Groenwald had called on the best hunter with the best hounds in the whole territory to help him catch the wild beast that had killed his sheep.

Many a time at night I'd heard those dog voices on a hot coon trail along the bayou or the swamp or in the rocky hill country above Old Man Pad-dler's Abraham Lincoln-style cabin.

Jay is a big long-bodied, hundred-pound blue-tick with a deep-voiced hollow bawl. Bawler is a lanky black and tan only about half as big as Jay. She has a high-pitched wail that sends cold chills up and down your spine when she's excited and going strong on a hot trail.

"Let's go join the hunt!" Poetry exclaimed to me. And I answered, "Sure! Let's go."

Dad stopped us, though, by saying, "It's an or-ganized hunt. The men'll have guns, and they won't want any boys along."

It didn't feel good to be stopped, but we weren't the only boys who didn't get to go. Circus Brown, the best athlete and the acrobat of our gang, Dan Brown's only son, didn't get to go either.

In a few jiffies there he was, coming through the orchard toward us. On a leash running all

14

around him in a lot of excitement was his new
hound pup he had named "Ichabod," one of the
cutest black and tan hound pups you ever saw.

"The hounds are coming this way," Poetry cried.
"Listen! That means Old Stubtail came this direction last night after he killed the lambs. I'll bet
he's got his home down in the swamp or maybe
along the bayou!"

"Or in the cave," a voice behind us piped up. It
was Little Jim, the littlest member of the gang,
who had come without making any noise.

Say, Old Bawler and Jay were *really* coming our
way. Already they were in the lane at the south
side of our pasture. Over the fence, through our
pasture and watermellon patch, and straight for
the pignut trees at the north end of our garden.

That was enough to scare me. It meant that last
night after Old Stubtail, as Circus called him, had
had his lamb dinner at Groenwald's he had come
across our south pasture, through our farmyard,
and had been only a hundred yards from our henhouse and—

I got my thoughts interrupted then by the
hound pup on Circus' leash going simply wild with
excitement on account of Bawler was his mother,
and he wanted to get into the excitement, whatever it was.

Almost before anybody could have said Jack

Robinson his pup was at the end of his leash, pulling and tugging and struggling wildly and just as quick his collar was over his head and he was off toward the pignut trees to join in whatever kind of dog game his mother and Old Jay were playing.

And that's when I heard his hunting voice for the first time. It was a long, high-pitched wailing tremolo like the highest tone in the organ at our church. It was the longest wail I'd ever heard.

Now there were *three* hounds, and I think I never saw hunting dogs more excited. They were as excited as if it had been only a few hours or maybe only a few minutes since the big cat had gone through our orchard, for they were over in the orchard now, heading through it toward Poetry's dad's woods and the mouth of the branch beyond and the cave beyond that and Old Man Paddler's hills beyond that.

Dan Brown let out a yell when little Ichabod joined the chase and ordered him to stop, but Ichabod wouldn't. It was too much fun. He was also using his own sense of smell to tell him where to trail.

At the orchard fence, though, he scared up a rabbit and was off in a different direction, giving chase with an even more excited voice than before.

Bawler and Jay were quick *over* the orchard

fence on their way toward the Sugar Creek bridge, and Ichabod was heading toward the place where he'd last seen the rabbit, which was near the bee-hives in the orchard.

Circus made a dive for his hound when he circled near, grabbed him, and soon had him on leash again. He also gave him a good scolding, saying, "Don't you *ever* do that again! *Never* leave one trail for another—do you hear!"

Well, it was a long, hard chase for Dan Brown and his hounds. Somewhere in the hills in dry ragged outcroppings above Old Man Paddler's cabin, they lost the scent, and the hunt was over.

Thinking maybe Old Stubtail might come back to finish eating one of the lambs he'd killed, Dan Brown set a number three double-spring steel trap at the place in the fence where it was easy for a large cat to get through. He tied a feather on a string and hung it on an elderberry bush close to the trap so the wind would blow it. The cat, belonging to the same family as a house cat which will be drawn to anything like that, might see the feather, smell the bait near the trap, and get caught.

That night a farmer three miles down the creek lost a calf. The kill was the same kind: a broken neck *in front* of the shoulders, a hole *behind* the shoulder, and the heart and liver eaten out.

2

DAN BROWN tried the dogs again, and again they lost the trail in the hills above Old Man Paddler's cabin. He tried setting traps in every place that looked like good cat cover, but always it was no use. Old Stubtail was too smart to let himself get caught.

Then for a week there were no more kills—not even one—and it began to look like the big cat had moved to safer territory, maybe clear out of the county.

Two more weeks passed and still nobody reported any livestock being killed, so we all began to breathe easily. Dan Brown felt sure it was so when, one day, Harm Groenwald reported some wild animal had eaten a batch of special cat poison he'd put out in what looked like a likely place. It was after that the reports of raiding stopped altogether.

The Sugar Creek county fair week came, and most of us got to go for a day. It was always fun to go where there were so many people, so many exhibits to see—and some of the gang won prizes for their lambs or pigs or calves.

It was while we were watching a clown doing acrobatic stunts on a flying trapeze that Little Jim, the littlest member of our gang, got the idea he wanted to be a trapeze artist. There was almost no living with him for awhile. He'd talk it, sing it, pretend it, and also act out all kinds of dangerous acrobatic stunts when he was with us.

Once at our house he leaped up, caught hold of the two-by-four at the east end of our grape arbor, swung his feet up and over, and "skinned the cat." Before I could stop him, he had stood up and actually walked across from one end to the other.

"You're getting reckless," I told him. "You better not ever do that again!"

"Better stick to piano playing," Poetry, who was there, told him. As you know, Little Jim was the best boy pianist in the whole Sugar Creek territory, his mother being the organist and pianist in our church.

"My fingers get enough exercise," Little Jim said. "More than enough. I'm going to be an athlete all over."

And we couldn't stop him. He taught himself to do the cartwheel, shinny up trees faster'n anything, and chin himself fifteen times. Once in our haymow he climbed high above the hay and walked across the highest beam, a proud grin on his face. I'd walked that beam myself a few times, and with the hay below it wasn't too dangerous. But it seemed ten times worse for Little Jim to do it.

But Little Jim was good, and getting better. The only thing was, we didn't dare tell him not to climb up to any dangerous place, or he'd be sure to want to do it.

It was while he was still working hard learning to become a stunt man that we read a story in the *Sugar Creek Times* of sheep killings, lost calves, and even a colt in Parke County, almost a hundred miles from where we lived. And *that*, we decided, explained what had happened to Old Stubtail. He'd left our neighborhood for safer territory.

Because Dan Brown's hounds were known all over the country and because he had had better success than most anybody running down "cats," as he called them, he got a phone call to bring Jay and Bawler and his traps to Parke County. Not only would he get a bounty for killing Old Stubtail but the farmers would make up a special purse of one hundred dollars for him.

Dan Brown, as you maybe know, used to be a drunkard. But wasn't anymore, because he had turned his life over to God to let Him run it, and whiskey and beer and other alcoholic drinks had gone out.

I never will forget what I heard him say once when he was telling Little Tom Till's infidel, drinking father what had happened to him. They'd been standing at the spring down near the creek at the time. Dan Brown had just handed old hook-nose John Till a drink of water, and Hooknose said, "No thanks, I like this better." And he pulled a flask of whiskey from his hip pocket, lifted it to his lips, and took a swig. Dan raised his voice and said sternly, "I *used* to do that, but when I let Christ into my life alcohol went out for good. I was like Old Bawler while I was training her to be a good coon hound. She kept getting off on rabbits, possums, skunk—anything except what I wanted her to trail. I finally got her trained, except for one thing. She'd always turn aside when she crossed a hot skunk track. I had to punish her again and again for that.

"God had to punish *me* too—plenty. But He finally won. Now, every time I'm tempted to leave *His* trail for me, to chase off after something He doesn't want, I think of Old Bawler and her pole-cat-chasing. Liquor," Dan Brown finished, as he took another sip of water from the spring, "is the worst skunk of all."

I saw old hook-nosed John Till's face turn black

with anger. He whirled around, lifted his flask, and drew on it long and hard till it was empty. Then he said, "You can keep your sermons for yourself!" He flung the bottle toward the board fence behind which I was hiding at the time. It hit with a crash, broke into a thousand pieces of fine glass, and scared me half to smithereens.

But I never forgot—and never would.

Everybody around Sugar Creek knew what a difference Dan's becoming a Christian had made in the Brown family, and people never got over talking about it. Dan never did either, and sometimes he'd get an invitation to speak in a church or a school assembly or even in the county jail.

His talk would nearly always be called "Trailing Trash." "Whenever a dog leaves a trail for something the hunter doesn't want, it's called trailing trash," he would tell them. "I've trailed a lot of trash in my day—staying away from church without a good reason I could give to God, using profanity, being unfair to my wife or children, buying booze instead of shoes."

He certainly was well trained, all right, just like he'd trained his hounds. Old Jay and Bawler were so good and so well trained that sometimes Dan'd get a call to another state to bring his dogs and track down something or other that was killing sheep or cattle or too many deer.

Once a wealthy rancher from out west had come to Sugar Creek in his private plane and flown Circus' dad to his ranch to help him catch a mountain lion that was raiding his corral and stealing one lamb after another.

The morning Dan left for Parke County he stopped his pickup at our house to ask Mom to be sure to phone his wife every day several times. "We're getting a new baby at our house next month," I heard him say.

I was standing near the mailbox admiring Dan's long-nosed, long-eared, sad-faced hounds, Jay and Bawler, leashed in the back of the pickup. I noticed Ichabod was in the front seat with Circus who was holding onto his collar, trying to calm him down.

"You going too?" I asked Circus.

"Just this far," Circus said. "Ichy'd get his eyes scratched out and his ears slit to ribbons if he ever got into a fight with Old Stubtail. He's got to get experience catching coons first — and they're bad enough."

Pretty soon Circus was out of the pickup, with Ichabod putting up a noisy fuss to get in the back with his mother and Old Jay. But Circus didn't let him. "You can't go!" Circus scolded him and held onto his collar. "You stay home with me and be a good boy, and we'll let you catch a baby coon.

There's a nest of them down in the old elm above the papaw bushes. Understand?"

Ichabod didn't understand, and he kept on trying to get up where his mother was.

Just before Dan drove away I heard Mom say to him, "Bill's expecting a new cousin in Memory City before long. I've promised to be there to help celebrate. But it'll be several weeks yet, and you'll be home before that, so I can phone your wife every day you're gone."

But it *wasn't* several weeks. It wasn't even several *days*. The very next morning early the phone rang. It wasn't an emergency ring, but it *was* an emergency. Wally, my city cousin, was going to get his new baby sister or brother that very day, and Mom was supposed to come right away to help celebrate.

In less time almost than it takes me to write it, Mom had Charlotte Ann and herself ready and in the car. Dad was also in and they were ready to start.

Even though my baby cousin was going to be born that day in Memory City, I wasn't going to get to go. I had to stay home to finish the morning chores, to hoe the potatoes in the little patch that belonged to me, and to do the chores in the evening just in case for some reason Dad didn't get home in time to do them with me.

24

Old Jersey, our one milk cow, had to be milked twice a day. And the other stock had to be fed, including the six little pigs in the straw with their mother—although they could feed themselves.

Dad was behind the steering wheel of the car when he gave me my final orders. "I'd rather you didn't use your new rifle for target practice while I'm away."

"Yes sir," I said, and felt sad and glad at the same time: glad all over that I had a rifle of my own, and sad that Dad didn't think I was big enough to know how to use it all by myself.

"Another thing," Dad said above the whirring of the car motor, "in case of rain, close all the windows of the house. And as soon as the chickens are all in tonight, shut the henhouse door."

Mom had a few instructions too. "Your dinner is on the stove. Just warm it up. And while I'm gone, you and your father wash the dishes at least once a day."

They were off in a whirl of dust, leaving me to myself for what would probably be a whole day. It might even be after dark before Dad could get back.

I watched the car until it disappeared, and I watched the cloud of dust it had raised until the wind had blown it into nothing in the direction of Bumblebee Hill. Then I went into the house to the phone by the east window and turned the crank on the phone, two shorts and a long.

When Poetry's mother answered, I asked for Poetry himself. She called him in a loud mother-like voice and while I was waiting for him to come from wherever he was, his mother said to me, "I suppose you want my son to come over and keep you company while you're all alone today?"

"How'd you know?" I asked. And she answered, "A little bird told me."

I knew she probably meant she'd accidentally had her phone receiver off the hook when Mom was talking to Wally's father long distance.

When Poetry answered, he was very mysterious in his tone of voice. "Listen," he hissed, "I've got a secret. You'd never guess what."

"What?" I asked. And he answered in his still-mysterious voice, "I'll tell you this afternoon while down at the mouth of the branch, fishing."

"I've gotta hoe potatoes," I objected. "I'm not sure I'll let me go fishing."

"Your folks gone to Memory City, aren't they?"

"Yes, but—"

"All right then. I'll meet you with my secret at two o'clock. At the mouth of the branch."

"Why don't you come over right now?" I asked. "You could help me hoe the potatoes and we could get done faster and catch more fish sooner."

His answer didn't have any mystery in its tone of voice. It was, "I have a father."

We set the date for two o'clock then, and I started off on the run to finish the morning chores and to get the potato patch cleaned of every weed there was.

It felt good to really work, something for some reason I was beginning to like to do.

Maybe it was 'cause Mom and Dad had been bragging on me a little for being so thoughtful around the house and farm. Or else it was because, I'd proved for the past six weeks that I *could* be thoughtful, that I *could* get up in the morning without being called three times, that I *could* actually take my Saturday night bath without being told to four times—such things as that. To reward me, Dad had bought for me the beautiful new .22 Savage rifle.

To earn it, Dad had told me I'd have to prove I could take responsibility. I would have to show him I could act even older than my age. Also I'd had to learn by heart, word for word "The Ten Commandments of Hunting Safety" and to pass a written examination on it. A *written* examination, mind you, just like a boy has to in school!

But I'd passed with an almost perfect grade, and it had felt so good to actually *be* good that I was sort of keeping on, like a wound-up clock.

I decided to surprise my parents by cleaning up the yard first, before starting on the potatoes.

Several times when I stopped to rest and to go into the house for cookies or something, I looked longingly up at my .22, took it down several times, and wished Dad hadn't thought to tell me not to do any target practice while he was away.

Once, just to be sure I had not broken one of the most important rules of hunting safety, I opened the breach to see if I had left it unloaded. I was glad I had because one of the rules is never to leave a loaded gun unattended. I patted its shining walnut stock, stroked its blue steel barrel and said to it, calling it by the name I'd given it the day Dad bought it for me, "Betty Lizzie, one of these days you're going to come in handy. You'll maybe save my life in an emergency."

Then I went outdoors, picked up my bait can which would have been perfect for setting on a fence post and using for a target, took my long cane fishing pole and went out the front gate, passing THEODORE COLLINS on our mailbox. My bare feet went *plop-plop-plopety-plop-plop* in the dust of the graveled road on the way to meet my best friend who said he was bringing a mystery with him.

Since there wasn't any wildcat in the territory for a boy to be scared of the gang'd have to think up something interesting to talk about and to be a little worried about. Life's a lot more interesting if there *is* a mystery around or something exciting or a bit dangerous. For that reason, I kind of hated to think of Old Stubtail being so far away. A boy ought to have a chance to find out how good a shot he is and whether a bullet from a .22 could really kill a wildcat.

"Ho hum," I yawned to myself, and as I lazied along, I wondered if maybe I'd catch a fish or two before Poetry came. For some reason, I must have eaten too much of the boiled dinner Mom had left for me. I had warmed it up and eaten several large helpings of it. I certainly felt sleepy. In a few minutes I'd be at the mouth of the branch where there was a nice grassy place to stretch out on and take a nap while the wriggling, twisting angleworms tempted the fish to bite away down in the water on the end of my hook.

It certainly was quiet around Sugar Creek—too quiet for a boy.

Too, *too* quiet.

Almost as quiet as it is sometimes just before there is a big thunderstorm. As quiet as a cat sneaking up on a mouse.

How was I to know, as I baited my hook and tossed my line out into the lazy water, that even though nobody around Sugar Creek had reported any killings by Old Stubtail and even though some farmers in Parke County a hundred miles away had lost a few sheep and other livestock—how was I to know that that great big twenty-eight toothed, savage-tempered wildcat was still hanging around our territory? How was I to know that that sleepy afternoon was to be the beginning of more excitement than the gang had had in a long time?

That very afternoon!

3

As you maybe know, the mouth of the branch is not far from the sycamore tree and the cave where we'd had so many interesting experiences. I was glad when I got there that Poetry wasn't already there with his mystery because sometimes his mysteries turned out to be just his imagination stretched too far.

I wasn't in the mood to get excited about anything. It was too lazy a day for even a hungry fish to bite, I thought. I did put on several of the juiciest worms I had in my bait can, and pretty soon I was stretched out in the sun watching my bottle-cork bobber lying lazily on the foam-specked water.

I waited and waited for a bite, waited also for Poetry. It wasn't two o'clock yet by nearly fifteen minutes. My bobber was as lifeless as I felt, and the slow-moving foam clusters kept on drifting past it while a half-dozen devil's darning needle dragonflies skimmed all around it over the water like baby-sized, four-winged airplanes looking for a landing field. They kept coming and going, making me dizzy almost.

I was too drowsy to care whether I got any bites, and I hoped my barrel-shaped best friend would stay away until I'd had a nice little snooze.

My nodding head woke me up just enough to remind me I'd better set my pole good and tight in case I actually *did* go to sleep. In case some lazy fish down there in the water somewhere should wake up and yawn, swallow the juicy wriggling cluster of angleworms with my sharp-barbed hook in them, feel the barb, and suddenly wake up and start running wildly in every direction all around and out into deeper water—if *that* should happen while I was sleeping, the great big savage fish might pull my pole in after it.

I was on my back now, my head resting on a stone pillow which I had made more comfortable by covering it with my jacket. I pulled my straw hat over my eyes to shade them from the sun and its light, yawned several noisy yawns, sighed several sighs, and let my lazy thoughts drift away into nothing. It seemed I was like Wynken, Blynken and Nod sailing about in the sky in a wooden shoe in the poem every boy knows, which was written by Eugene Field and is in one of the readers in our school library.

I was in the wooden shoe now with Wynken, Blynken and Nod, sailing higher and higher, past the moon and stars. I was fishing in a sea of dew.

Was I actually asleep? I wondered.

Just then I became aware of the stone pillow under my head. And one of the Bible stories I'd heard Dad read—and which you already know about—started roaming about in my mind. If I was dreaming, I thought, I certainly wasn't red-haired Bill Collins who didn't have any brother to fight with but had only a red-haired city cousin who had a city-bred, ill-mannered mongrel of a dog that wasn't afraid of anything but would rush in where an ordinary dog would be scared to even bark.

In my dream, if it was a dream, it seemed I was Jacob who had had a quarrel with his brother, Esau, and I had run away to keep from getting killed. It was night and I was in a very rocky place where there were wildcats hiding in caves and going up and down a stone stairway made of gold like a city department store escalator.

Then in my dream, which I was sure wasn't a dream, I heard a Voice from the top of the ladder, calling down to me, saying, "The ground on which you are lying—I am going to give it to you. . . ."

It was a very strong, very kind, very deep, echoing voice, different from any I had ever heard. It seemed like it was the voice of God who had made all the wonderful things in nature—the creek and the birds, the rocks and rills, the woods and templed hills, all the boys there are in the world—and even the girls.

I had *felt* the Voice many a time in my heart but had never before *heard* it. It sounded like organ music in the Sugar Creek Church, also like water in the riffles and slow, friendly thunder after a storm. It made me think of a slow hand stroking the soft fur of a kitten. . . .

And then is when I woke up.

I had heard a strange sound close by that scared me all to smithereens.

There was a fast wind ruffling the surface of the creek. My brown bottle-cork bobber was zigzagging around like I was getting a whopper of a bite, and in the direction of the swamp there was the excited rumble of actual thunder. The sun was smothered under a cover of worried, dark brown clouds, and there was the smell of rain in the air. I must have slept quite awhile, I thought.

Then is when I heard another sound and saw what had made it. On the trunk of the big elm overhanging the water was a great big furry animal of some kind. It looked like a giant-sized tiger cat ten times as big as Mixy, the Collins family's black and white house cat. Only it didn't have any nice,

34

long, bushy tail. It had a stub about eight inches long.

I guess I never was so wide awake so fast in my life. The fierce-looking animal was crouching in my direction, snarling, and had one wide front foot on the bloody carcass of what was left of a half-eaten rabbit.

I saw the angry gray-green eyes glaring at me like I had interrupted his dinner, heard him spitting and hissing like Mixy spits and hisses when she's angry or interrupted in her eating.

In that fleeting flash of a few seconds, I saw the brown stripes on its forehead, the long gray-white whiskers, the whitish chin and throat. The one claw-filled huge paw holding down the remains of the bunny looked like it was powerful enough to rip a dog's ears to shreds with one fierce, fast thrust.

I was sitting up at the time, which means I must have awakened with such a start I was halfway up before I realized it—like a boy sometimes does even when he is home and safe in a nice warm bed.

Now, I managed to think, would be a good time to see how fast I could run toward Theodore Collins' house and a good time to try out a .22 Savage on a savage wild animal. It certainly wouldn't be disobeying Dad to kill Old Stubtail because that wouldn't be target practice at all.

I was on my feet in a flash, ready to start on a speedy sprint toward the branch bridge and across it on the way to get Betty Lizzie.

Then's when I caught a glimpse of my fishing line cutting a wide circle in the water, saw and heard the cane pole bouncing like I had on a fish as big as a wildcat.

I quick made a dive for the pole, grabbed it, felt the wild-running fish on the other end of the line, forgot about being scared of the wildcat, and in a few fast, not-very-skillful movements had landed a whopper of a large-mouth bass. I remembered while I was doing it that fish bite better when it's raining or going to rain.

Right then also I heard another roll of thunder —not in the distance but a lot closer. I hurried to get the bass off the hook and onto the stringer I'd brought—not being able to feel proud of myself for catching him on account of the wildcat not more than twenty-five feet from me on the over-hanging elm trunk. Anybody knows a boy can't feel proud and yet be scared half to death at the same time.

I knew, of course, that wildcats eat mice and rabbits and small birds but wouldn't attack any human being unless they were cornered or thought they were. I certainly wasn't going to get close enough to the base of the overhanging tree to make

Old Stubtail think I was after him, that he was cornered and to run the risk of having him spring at me. But why let him scare me out of what few wits I had? I didn't *have* to let him keep me from catching another big fish—or setting my pole again. I quick baited the hook with a half-dozen of the biggest, juiciest, liveliest worms in the target-practice can.

First, I tied the free end of my stringer onto a willow near the shore and eased the whopper of a bass I'd already caught, into the water at the edge, so he'd stay alive. In another jiffy now my pole would be set and I'd be flying home for Betty Lizzie. I might even get the savage-looking wild-cat killed before Poetry came.

Then's when I heard a boy's squawky, duck-like voice calling from the direction of the branch bridge. A second later the boy behind the voice broke through the bushes, and it was Poetry running like a barrel with legs on it, carrying a large rectangular brown envelope.

Then, also, is when it began to rain and the wind blew hard. "Come on!" he yelled to me. "Let's get to the cave or we'll be drowned! There's a terrible storm coming up!" He shoved the brown envelope inside his shirt to keep it from getting wet.

"Look!" I cried to him, and pointed with my arm toward the overhanging tree. "There's a wildcat

37

up there! Old Stubtail's back again! He's up there eating a rabbit!"

"Where?" he asked and looked toward where I was pointing.

"Right up there—right—right—!"

But there wasn't any wildcat with fierce face and savage claws glaring down at us. And there wasn't any half-eaten bloody carcass of a rabbit.

What, I thought, *on earth!"*

Poetry irked me into getting almost fighting mad at him when he said sarcastically, "Oh yeah! A wildcat or a wild *idea?"*

Then it did begin to rain, and there was a roaring in the trees overhead and all around. A blinding lightning flash and an explosion of thunder at the same time, ten times louder than a rifle shot, screamed in my mind for me to get out of there in a hurry—away from any tall trees which are dangerous to be under when there's an electric storm.

Gritting my teeth at being made fun of by my best friend and having my word doubted, I cried to him, "There *was* a wildcat up there eating a rabbit! He was spitting and hissing and his right front paw had curving claws that could scratch a dog's eyes out and tear his ear to shreds in one fierce, fast stroke!"

But where *was* the furry animal that'd been

38

there only a few excited minutes ago? I knew I'd seen him. *Knew* it!

There wasn't time now to argue, and it wouldn't do any good anyway. We had to get to the cave quick, or get as wet as or wetter than if we'd fallen in the creek.

Our four bare feet flew in the path we'd run in a thousand times in our lives, in fact almost a thousand times that very summer, toward the sycamore tree and the cave.

The wildcat'd get wet too, I thought. And in my mind's eye I saw our old black and white cat at home. Whenever she was outdoors and it started to rain, she would come to fast cat life and run like a scared rabbit to the house or to the toolshed or streak like a four-legged arrow across the barnyard to the hole that goes under the barn.

"Maybe wildcats are like pussycats," I thought out loud. "Maybe Old Stubtail hurried down the tree to get in out of the rain."

"Yeah," Poetry's voice puffed his reply as he lumbered along behind me. "Maybe he's outrun us and is already in the cave!"

"Cave!" my mind and my voice screamed it at the same time.

It was an exciting idea—and a scary one. Maybe Old Stubtail *had* gone to the cave to get in out of the rain. Maybe he had made it his home already and had his den there somewhere. Maybe after he would lose the dogs up in the hills, he'd circle back through the swamp and hide in his secret place in the cave!

It took two fast-running boys only a half-dozen wet minutes to get to the sycamore tree with its white and purple and gray bark, which I didn't even bother to notice, and inside the black open mouth of the cave. There we stopped, panting for breath, and looked back out at the rain that was coming down in sheets, heard the roaring wind and saw the trees whipping hard.

There were a lot of things on my mind right then: the strange and very wonderful dream of the golden escalator leading up to the skies, the Voice I'd heard in the dream, the whopper of a bass I'd caught and which, right that minute, was on the end of the stringer in the creek, the angry eyes of the wildcat, Poetry's doubting my words, calling them a wild idea, the storm that had driven us here, the wildcat being gone when I'd pointed out to Poetry where he was.

It certainly was storming hard: wind, jagged lightning, deafening thunder, and blinding sheets of rain.

I tried telling Poetry over again about what I'd seen but he still doubted my word. "Old Stubtail's down in Parke County— don't you remember? Circus' father and Old Jay and Bawler left yesterday to go down and catch him."

"But I saw him when I woke up!" I protested. I told Poetry about my going to sleep, and all of a sudden waking up with the wind blowing and low clouds scudding across the sky. I told him about the whopper of a bass I'd caught, and the wildcat eating the rabbit.

But his mind was like an up umbrella in the rain. My words fell on him and rolled off. "All right," I said, "call me a liar."

"You're not a liar," he defended me. "You just have an elastic imagination. You *thought* you saw it. You just said yourself you'd been asleep and the wind woke you up!"

I *had* just said that to him, but I certainly didn't expect him to take my words, make a whip out of them, and give me a switching with them.

All the time while the wind was whipping the trees outside the cave and the thunder and lightning were acting like they were mad at each other and at the whole world I was thinking about Old Stubtail I *knew* I'd seen and heard. I wondered what had become of him. There wasn't much of anything we could do in the cave while we waited for the storm to stop, and it was pretty dark on account of there wasn't any sunshine outside.

In my mind was the new idea that had come to

41

me a little while before that Old Stubtail *might* have run to the cave to get in out of the rain! He *might* be here right now, not more than a few feet from us!

All of a sudden, I heard something behind me that started my hair to crawling on the back of my neck.

"Hear that!" I whispered huskily. "That's him! That's Old Stubtail! He's back in the cave somewhere behind us."

4

I was scared now even worse than I had been back at the base of the leaning elm, on whose trunk I'd seen the wildcat.

It's not nearly as frightening to *see* a dangerous wild animal when you're quite a ways away from it as it is to be in a dark cave and *hear* one behind you somewhere—and you can't see it.

The roar of the storm outside didn't make it any easier for us to hear what we were trying to hear.

Scratch . . . scratch. . . . That's what I thought I'd heard.

I'd never seen Poetry so calm at a time like that. "We'll find out in one minute if there's anything back in there anywhere," he said.

Of course we knew the other end of the cave came out away up in the hills in the basement of Old Man Paddler's cabin, but what we were hearing was right close by, *very* close. Not more than six feet from us, it seemed.

In a jiffy, Poetry had his waterproof matchbox

43

out, the one he nearly always carried with him. He struck a match and lit one of the candles we kept on a shelf in a holder. We'd lit candles there many a time when we'd had gang meetings.

"Now," he said, "we'll—"

Then we *did* hear something for sure.

"It's behind the wall here somewhere," I said. "It's the wildcat! He's got his den here in the cave! That's why he wasn't on the tree when I tried to show you he was! He knew the storm was coming and made a beeline for here!"

Just saying it made it seem actually the truth, and I was cringing plenty.

Poetry's face in the light of the candle showed he was a little afraid himself, but he wasn't the kind of boy to admit it. "Let's have a look," he said, and held the candle close to the wall where we'd heard the sound. Then he let out a heavy, disgruntled sigh and said, "Well that's that. There's a leak in the cave roof. See the water dripping?"

I'd already seen, and my ears were already hearing *Drip . . . drip . . . drip* instead of *scratch . . . scratch . . . scratch*.

Well, while we were waiting for the storm to subside, we used the light of the candle to help us see to put together Poetry's space patrol periscope which was his mystery and was in the brown envelope. First we took it out of the envelope, cleaned the two mirrors, one at either end like the directions for assembling it said, and step by step put it together. It'd be fun to use it, being able to see around corners without being seen, look over the tops of people's heads to watch a parade, or over the stone fence at the cemetery while we ourselves would be on the other side. There'd be a lot of uses for it.

I was still irked at my best friend, though, for not believing me about the whopper of a cat I'd seen. Of course, I'd seen him. I hadn't been just dreaming, I was sure, 'cause I'd also caught a whopper of a bass, and I *knew* I wasn't dreaming when I'd done that. I had proof of it, on the stringer tied to the willow down by the mouth of the branch.

I began to feel a little better toward Poetry, though, while we worked together on the periscope. *After all he is my best friend,* I thought. We'd had more fun and trouble together than any two of the rest of the gang.

"As soon as this storm is over," he announced, "we'll go back to where you saw your little kitty and look for clues. If we find blood on the tree trunk where he was chewing on the rabbit, we'll know you weren't asleep."

And then I was mad again.

I gritted my teeth and said, "OK, chum, have it

your way. We'll find the blood. It'll be there, all right."

As soon as we were sure the storm was over, we went out in the rain-washed air and splashed our way down the muddy path to the mouth of the branch where I'd seen the "kitty" and where my whopper of a bass was on the stringer, the other end of which was tied to the willow not far from the base of the leaning elm.

Poetry worked his way carefully along the trunk of the tree so as not to fall off the slippery wet bark, and I stood grinning expecting him any minute to find a little blood or some bits of rabbit fur to prove I was right.

"Nothing here," he called back. "Not even a scratch on the bark, not a single claw mark."

I called up to him, "The rain washed the blood off, and if there was any rabbit fur, it washed off into the creek and floated down stream!"

At least he'd believe me about the whopper of a bass I'd caught.

I'd been bragging about that to him, too.

"OK," I said "Come on down and I'll let you carry my bass home."

I caught hold of the end of the stringer, not untying it first, 'cause I wanted to hold up the whopper for Poetry to see without running the risk of him getting away.

Then I felt a sinking sensation in the pit of my stomach. There wasn't any big large-mouth bass on the end of the stringer! There wasn't *anything*. The stringer was empty. *Empty!*

"What on earth!" I exclaimed

"I will be in a minute!" Poetry called down to me from the place on the tree trunk where the wildcat had been and now wasn't. We stood for a few seconds looking at my empty stringer. I could feel what he was thinking before he let out a grunt and exploded with: "The wildcat that wasn't there ate a whopper of a bass that wasn't there that had been caught by a red-haired, freckled-faced boy that wasn't *all* there!"—meaning he thought I wasn't quite bright.

Before I could even start to prove to him I was, he grunted again, caught the stringer by the empty other end, studied it a second, and said in his duck-like voice, "Or maybe the *bunny* that hadn't even been there ate the *fish* that wasn't there that was caught by the *boy* that wasn't—"

That was as far as he got. I chopped his sentence in two by exploding at him with: "If the barrel-shaped fat boy had been there, there wouldn't have been room enough for anything else!"

It wasn't a very kind thing to say on account of extra-heavy people shouldn't be made fun of unless they do it themselves. My parents had taught me

47

that. They were always extra careful not to hurt anybody's feelings.

I untied the stringer from the willow, hardly able to see it on account of the crazy old tears that were in my eyes. Now I was *really* angry at my best friend—not so much because he was making fun of me but because I couldn't prove to him there *had* been a wildcat eating a bunny which there actually *had* been and because there wasn't even any whopper of a large-mouth bass on the stringer which I myself had caught and put there.

Well, it was time for me to go home and start the evening chores and it was also time for Poetry to go home. I knew it was for sure when I heard from away up near their house his mother's voice calling in a high-pitched tremolo that sounded almost as much like Ichabod's long-toned wail as Ichabod's real voice. The way the long-toned, high-pitched cry echoed down through the woods sent cold chills up and down my spine. For a second it seemed like I was running with the gang, following the hounds on a hot wildcat trail.

Always mischievous-minded, Poetry swung his periscope up to his eyes and looked in the small round hole at the bottom, saying at the same time, "Maybe I can see your little kitty by looking in here."

Of course he couldn't.

His mother called again, and her tremolo sounded like she was really on a hot trail this time. Poetry let out a yell back and was quick on a fat run in the wet path toward the branch bridge and on toward his home.

I myself went on toward the Theodore Collins' house, carrying the sad-looking empty stringer and my long cane fishing pole—and with an empty feeling in my heart.

It was a sad, wet walk, the rain having poured down so hard little rivulets were running in the graveled road, and there was muddy water everywhere. There were green leaves all over blown from the trees and quite a few fallen branches. The storm must have been even worse than it had seemed while we were in the cave.

Inside the house I took a quick half-sad, half-glad look up at Betty Lizzie on her rack above the closed east door. I was certainly glad I had left that door closed, also the window by the phone, 'cause the wind had come from the east and we'd have had water inside all over the floor. It wasn't any credit to me, though, on account of the door and that east window had already been closed when I'd gone fishing.

I took a quick look-run-see all over the house upstairs and down to be sure there wasn't any water on the floor anywhere or on the beds and felt a little better that there wasn't any.

Just that second while I was still upstairs, our phone rang one long and one short. It was our ring.

That'll be Poetry, I thought. *He wants to make up. He's sorry he teased me.*

But instead it was long distance. Dad was calling from Memory City. The celebration at Wally's house hadn't started yet. There also had been a bad electric storm and several bridges were out. He wanted to know if I was all right.

I was glad to tell Dad I was and that the rain hadn't rained in the house anywhere.

Mom got on the phone then and told me I could either stay all night at Poetry's or he could come and stay with me because Dad was going to wait till morning to start home. There'd been a little change in their plans.

My heart was pounding harder than it seemed like it ought to, on account of I wasn't used to long-distance phone calls. But a little later when I hung up, I felt better inside—like I'd done something important or something.

I took up the receiver again, held it in my hand, took hold of the crank handle of the phone with my right hand and got ready to ring two shorts and a long to ask Poetry to come and stay all night at my house. I got the two shorts rung before I re-

membered I was still mad at him, and I quick
hung up. I didn't need any fat, barrel-shaped baby-
sitter to look after me. Any boy who was old
enough to own a rifle and could catch a whopper
of a bass and—my thoughts stopped bragging on
me just then when I remembered the bass had
been *off* the stringer instead of *on* it.

Had I actually been dreaming? I wondered for
the first time.

Right now, as I stood again in the kitchen looking up at Betty Lizzie, it seemed there had not
only been a wildcat on the leaning tree eating a
rabbit, a big bass running wild on the other end of
my line but there had also been a wooden shoe as
big as a boat. I was in it sailing in a sea of dew
past the moon, and there had been a real escalator
with angels and wildcats riding up and down on it.

I didn't know what to believe.

But I *did* have to get the chores done, so I put
myself to work doing them.

My good sense, if I really had any, told me the
wooden-shoe boat and the angels on the escalator
had been only a dream, but the wildcat and the
bunny and the whopper of a large-mouth bass had
been for real.

* * *

When I went to bed in my upstairs south room
and lay there for a few minutes listening to the

51

whispering of the ivy leaves at the window and at the different night sounds in the woods, I was feeling quite a bit better in my mind. There was an ache in my heart, though, that my best friend hadn't believed me, and also that he hadn't called up to tell me he was sorry and that he *did* believe me.

I kept feeling something pulling at me to get out of bed, go down to the phone and ring two shorts and a long for Poetry to come over and stay with me. It was still early enough, and there was moonlight enough for him to bike his way over.

But I was stubborn in my mind at him, so I lay there on my soft white pillow and felt disgusted and worried a little. I wondered if any of the usual night sounds outside in the woods were unusual and were any of them being made by Old Stubtail who wasn't there.

In the middle of the night I was awakened by something. I didn't know what. I was so startled by whatever it was that I was sitting up in bed before I knew it, my heart pounding. Out in our chicken house there was such a squawking and cackling of both hens and roosters that I sprang from my bed to see what was the matter.

5

I HADN'T ANY SOONER sprung from my bed to see what was the matter out in our chicken house than I thought I heard a different kind of noise near Old Red Addie's apartment. I strained my eyes into the shadowy moonlight. The moon was in its last quarter and was only a silvery sliver hanging in the sky over the south pasture. The shadow of the barn covered all of Addie's house and lot and part of the chicken yard, so of course I couldn't really see what was the matter.

My mind's eye was seeing right through the chicken house wall and imagining a tufted-eared, leering-eyed, stub-tailed wildcat making short work of one of Mom's best laying hens. He might even be eating Old Bentcomb herself, my favorite white leghorn who always made her nest under a log up in our haymow. *She would make a tasty midnight snack for a hungry forty-five pound monster of a cat*, I thought.

Since Dad was away in Memory City and wouldn't be home till tomorrow some time, it'd be up to me, Bill Collins, to save our flock of hens. Also, it would give me a chance to use Betty Lizzie for something besides target practice.

The excitement in the chicken house seemed to

be getting noisier every second, which meant the whole flock was scared half to death about something.

I quick shoved myself into my overalls and, without bothering to put on a shirt over my pajama top scurried down the stairs and into and through the kitchen. I lighted my way with Dad's powerful three batteried flashlight.

It'd be silly to run any real risk, I thought. Old Stubtail, seeing me, might decide a red-haired boy would be just right for dessert. In a jiffy I had Betty Lizzie down and loaded. Then I eased my way out the back screen door and onto the boardwalk. I heard a sound that made me stop stockstill and cringe. It was the harsh, loud-voiced scream of a hen like she was being murdered.

That settled that. I, Bill Collins, the head of our empty house, was going into action. I held Betty Lizzie ready to shoot if I had to. Any minute now, some wild animal might come charging out of the hen house in my direction. Even in the middle of all that excitement I remembered rules seven and eight of the Ten Commandments for Hunting Safety: "Be sure of your target before you fire; never point a gun at anything you don't intend to shoot. Make sure of your partner's location before firing at anything. Don't hunt with more than one companion."

I was as far as the grape arbor when the harsh screaming hen's voice stopped like it had been choked off, which probably meant one of our hens was dead. But the excited cackling of the other chickens was still going on. I shot a beam from the flashlight straight toward the open hen house door. Open, mind you! And I had been ordered by Theodore Collins to close it!

I swung the flashlight back toward Addie's apartment and saw—or thought I saw, I couldn't tell for sure—a long, grayish-brown shadow stalking the pen, then a pair of fiery eyes, like two small flashlights shining back on me.

Just to be sure it *wasn't* two flashlights I turned mine off and the two went out. That meant I had actually seen two eyes of some kind of animal, reflected in my flashlight's light.

The grayish-brown shadowy thing came to life and went slinking along the garden fence toward the pignut trees and disappeared in the direction of Poetry's dad's woods.

I had seen Old Stubtail again! I was positively, absolutely sure of it! I, myself, Bill Collins, who was absolutely wide awake and not dreaming, had seen him with my own wide-awake eyes!

I hadn't realized that I had had Betty Lizzie pointed toward Addie's home and that I had swung the rifle in an arc following the flight of the shadow until my arms got tired of holding it in a pointed position.

I was trembling all over, but I was glad I hadn't pulled the trigger 'cause when I shot a beam of light in the direction of the pignut trees, it came to focus on Old Jersey, our milk cow, lying on her side there chewing her cud. We might have had a dead milk cow instead of a stub-tailed wildcat.

Well, there was still quite a lot of excitement in the hen house, so I decided to go over and shut the door, hoping the chickens would calm down a little and I could go back to bed and try to go to sleep.

First I shined my light through the open door and onto the four-foot-high roosts. "Listen, girls," I said in a half-comforting, half-scolding voice, "there's nothing more to worry about. Go on back to sleep! Old Stubtail's gone, and I'm going to shut your door and latch it."

But the whole flock seemed still to be nervous. Maybe it was because my light was bothering them, I thought. I turned it off and spoke again: "Calm down! There's nothing to be afraid of! Here, I'll prove it to you!"

I swung the light in a circle all around the ceiling and the roosts and onto the dirt floor under the old walnut table on which Mom had a few nests in little square boxes, and—

Then, is when I saw what was causing all the excitement. There, in a corner under the table, was a long gray-haired animal the size of a house cat with a long grayish-brown, naked tail. Its head was long and slender, its eyes beady, its large ears naked, and it was gnawing away on a bloody-necked white leghorn pullet.

"Possum!" I exclaimed. It wasn't a very big one and wasn't anything to be scared of—not for a boy with a gun. The gang had caught quite a few of them when we'd been hunting with Circus' dad's hounds. They hardly ever trailed one but *sometimes* did and got scolded for it if they had already been on a coon trail and had gotten off. I had even picked up a half-dozen possums myself by their long prehensile tails.

I shined Dad's flashlight full into Opi's grinning face—Opi being the name the gang had for any possum we happened to see or catch. True to a possum's nature at a time like that, he curled himself up into a ball, opened the lips of his long-nosed mouth, showing a long row of pretty, white teeth, and lay on his side, absolutely still.

I quick stooped, lifted him by his tail, carried him outside.

He didn't seem to like that 'cause he came to excited life for a jiffy, struggled to get his head up to bite my hand, then gave up again and went back to his pretended sleep.

It was only a possum and it wasn't possum hunting season, anyway, so I carried him to the orchard fence, dropped him over on the other side, and ordered him, "You stay out of our chicken house, do you hear!"

And that was that.

I went back, got what was left of Opi's midnight lunch, carried it to the orchard fence, and tossed it over where it fell under one of Dad's Early Elberta peach trees. Tomorrow I would bury it somewhere so the bluebottle flies wouldn't come and lay their eggs all over it. Even though I knew that the screwworms that would hatch from the bluebottle eggs were what Dad called "scavengers" and if given enough time would eat up the whole carcass, the larvae would grow into more bluebottle flies— and there were already too many.

Besides, I remembered that sometimes bluebottle flies laid their eggs in a cut or open sore of farm animals and the larvae ate the living tissues as well as the dead and caused a lot of deaths in cattle country, especially in the southern part of the United States.

So it's a good thing to kill or trap every bluebottle fly you can. Don't even let even a housefly live if you can help it.

Back to the chicken house door I went again and shut it tight and bolted it.

Still worried about what I'd seen—or *thought* I'd seen—at Addie's gate, I shot my light out there again, when what to my wondering eyes should appear but two fiery eyes again. Then something with black and white fur—and it was Mixy nosing around the gate and arching her lazy back against the post.

What a disappointment!

First I had thought there was a wildcat in the chicken house, and it had turned out to be a naked-eared, naked-tailed, long-nosed possum eating a leghorn pullet. And the wildcat I thought I'd seen at Addie's appartment gate had turned out to be a tame house cat that was wild only when in a hissing, spitting, scratching fight with a dog.

A few minutes before, when I had seen the fiery eyes and the gray-haired something-or-other stealing along the garden fence toward the pignut trees, I'd felt almost happy in spite of being scared. I had been sure there was a wildcat in the neighborhood, that Old Stubtail had come back from Parke County. In the afternoon when I was down at the mouth of the branch I *hadn't* been dreaming —not when I saw the actual rabbit being eaten by a tufted-eared, angry-eyed wild animal of the cat family.

I called Mixy and she came running toward me in a half awkward lope like cats do. I looked down at her blinking nonsensical eyes and growled at her grumpily: "It's your fault for scaring me! I'm disgusted!"

She meowed up at me a lazy meow, arched her back, pushed against my trowser leg and walked past. Then she started off on a cat trot toward the iron pitcher pump and the place where she knew her milk pan was, inviting me to come and feed her a midnight lunch.

I stood for a few seconds, thinking, feeling the cool night breeze on my pajama-clad arms. I sighed heavily, took a squint at the saucer-shaped moon, felt sleepy, and thought for a second about the poem, "Wynken, Blynken, and Nod." I yawned my way through one of the stanzas I had memorized, which was:

" 'Where are you going, and what do you wish?'
The old moon asked the three.
'We have come to fish for the herring fish
That live in this beautiful sea. . . .' "

There was another line that started out: "The old moon laughed and sang a song. . . ." I couldn't remember the rest of it. But as I kept on looking at the little sliver of a moon, it seemed it was shaped like a large silver mouth and it was laugh- at me for being such a scared goose.

Disappointed and sleepy, I carried Betty Lizzie into the house, unloaded her, went back upstairs, undressed and was soon in bed with Wynken, Blynken, and Nod.

I tried to remember the whole poem, saying it over in my mind. But I didn't get very far—only about as far as the place where it says: "Wynken and Blynken are two little eyes (fiery eyes, I thought).

And Nod is a little head. . . ."

The next thing I knew it was morning and the telephone downstairs was ringing one long and one short, the number everybody on the party line knew was ours.

6

FOR A FEW FAST JIFFIES I thought the phone ringing downstairs was Dad's alarm clock and that I'd
have quite a while to sleep before he'd start calling
me to wake up and come down to help him with
the chores.

I was back with Wynken, Blynken, and Nod in
a sea of dew when the phone rang again. In a flash
I realized nobody was home except myself, and
it'd be up to me to wake up and get up and go
down and answer the phone—which I did.

It wasn't anything very important, except I
was supposed to come over to Poetry's house for
dinner that day. Dad was invited, too.

"He's not home yet," I said to Poetry's mother.

"Not home, yet!" she exclaimed into her phone
speaker and into my receiver. "I thought he was
coming back last night!"

"He phoned me he'd not be here till today some-
time," I answered her.

Then her voice was astonished. "You mean you stayed all night alone there—all by yourself!"

Because I always liked to have a girl or a woman feel worried about me and think I was brave, I said: "Well, not exactly alone. I had our old cat, six little pigs, a possum, and a wildcat. But don't worry, I'm all right."

"Oh—you!" she exclaimed, then added, "I'll send Poetry over right away to help with the chores."

"No, *don't!*" I said. "I can get along very nicely —" I wanted to say, "I can get along very nicely *without* a fat boy who thinks I'm an idiot and won't believe what I say." But I remembered Dad's and Mom's ideal never to hurt people's feelings if you could help it, so I added into the phone, "Thank you very much for the invitation. I'll tell Dad as soon as he gets here."

I did feel a little better toward Mrs. Thompson's barrel-shaped son, though. So a little later when he actually did come over to help me with the chores, we started in acting like we liked each other again.

I told him all about Opi and the other excitement I'd had. Then I began to feel him doubting me again. Since he was so extra mischievous most of the time anyway, I could hardly tell whether he was joking when he said, "Yesterday it was a wildcat eating a rabbit. Last night it was a possum eating a chicken under the table in the hen house.

How come he didn't put his food *on* the table instead of *under* it! Show me what is left of the carcass and I'll believe you."

"Okay, smarty," I said. "Right this way." I led him to the orchard fence, looked over, and told him, "Right over there under the Early Elberta peach tree. I threw the carcass right over—right over—right—"

I stopped saying right 'cause I was wrong. There weren't any feathered remains of one of Mom's best laying pullets—not under the peach tree nor anywhere in a wide circle all around it.

What, I thought, *on earth!*

It was too much like yesterday when there hadn't been any wildcat or rabbit or any whopper of a bass. I'd been dreaming about that bass, and last night I'd been dreaming about herring in a sea of dew. It just didn't make sense.

Poetry stooped, picked up a white feather—a wing feather from one of Mom's hens, I supposed —tucked it under the band of his straw hat and squawked a stanza of a nonsensical song every boy knows:

> "Yankee Doodle went to town,
> Ridin' on a pony,
> Stuck a feather in his hat
> And called it macaroni."

He sang the poem as he said it, then asked sar-

castically, "How come he didn't call it bologna?"

Then he got a serious expression on his face. Maybe because he saw angry tears in my eyes or because he was my best friend—anyway he *had* been—he laid a fat arm across my shoulder and crooned, "If you say there was a possum, there was a possum. No reason why he couldn't have eaten the rest of the pullet or dragged it away somewhere."

I gulped, swung around, scooped up Mixy who was meowing at my feet, cuddled her a little, then started for the toolshed to get a spade. It'd be a wonderful morning to go fishing after yesterday's rain. It might be a good idea to get started before Dad came home.

The garden was too wet to hoe potatoes anyway. It's not good for potatoes to be hoed when the ground is soaking wet. We would leave a note for Dad on the kitchen table or somewhere telling him where we were, and telling him about our being invited to eat raspberry pie and roast beef at Poetry's house that noon.

That was another thing I found out: The gang's mothers had made it up between them to have Dad and me eat all our noon meals at their different houses everyday while Mom was in Memory City celebrating my cousin's new baby sister or brother.

65

It was fun digging the worms. The best place on our farm was not far from Addie's apartment. I used the spade, and Poetry used his hands to break up the big damp clods and pick up the worms.

"Angleworms or earthworms," Poetry began in what Dad would call a philosophical tone of voice, "are very helpful to the farmer. They eat dirt, swallowing it whole like fish eat earthworms. What they can't digest, they pile up in little piles around their burrows. In this way, they bring the deeper parts of the richer soil to the surface." It sounded like something he had memorized.

It surely felt good to have him seem like his good old mischievous self again and to feel that he liked me. I know what he was saying was the truth about earthworms on account of I had learned it myself listening to a 4-H club speaker at a special meeting different ones of our fathers had taken us to.

Addie, in her lot, seemed a lot more nervous than usual. She was squealing and complaining like she hadn't already had her breakfast of corn and tankage and a pail of separated milk from the separator.

Poetry stopped squawking about earthworms eating earth like fish eating fishing worms. Looking at Addie, he began quoting in a singsong tone the little ditty he had quoted to her one other time,

changing one of the lines a little to make it sound funnier:

"Six little pigs in the straw with their mother,
  Bright tails, curly eyes, tumbling on each other;
  Bring them apples from the orchard trees,
  And hear those piggies say, 'Please, please, please.'"

He started to singsong it again. Then he stopped stock-still, stared, and exploded: "Hey! I thought there were *six* little pigs! She's only got *five!*"

Of course he was joking, I thought. It was a good poem to quote, cute and just right for Addie to hear. She was so proud of her frisky little curly-tailed family. There were six in the poem and six in the pen.

Poetry plopped his bait can down where it fell on its side, and the wriggling squirming worms started to worm their way out into every direction there is. He quick set the can right side up, scooped up each runaway worm, and put it back in. There was a very sober expression on his face as he asked me, "How many pigs is she supposed to have?"

"Six," I answered. "Don't you remember? You saw them the morning after they were born, the day Chuck Hammer was here!"

His answer was with a grim voice, "She's got only five now. You sure one of 'em didn't die?"

I thought he was only pretending to be excited, so I said, "Oh, the other one'll be back in the apartment somewhere." But his excitement was like measles. It was contagious, and I was about to catch it from him. I was seeing again what I'd seen last night—two fiery eyes too wide apart and too high from the ground for them to have been Mixy's.

We left our spade and can of worms and in a jiffy were in the hog lot looking all over for a cute little curly-tailed rascal of a piggie that had probably hidden himself, or was taking a nap or wallowing in the mud all by himself.

We looked inside the apartment, under the straw, all around under the weeds in the lot, and there wasn't any little red-haired pig-child—not in the straw with its mother nor anywhere in the whole lot.

All of a sudden Poetry's eyes narrowed, and for an anxious jiffy we stared at each other. Then I heard him say excitedly, pointing down to a patch of chocolate-colored grass near the gate, "That looks like dried blood!"

I had been afraid to tell him what I thought I had seen at this very place last night, but now, I decided, was the time to tell him. I was sure now that those two fiery eyes belonged to Old Stubtail himself. He had really come back from Parke County.

"I saw Old Stubtail here last night," I said. "He was crouching right here. When I turned my flashlight on him, he slunk away."

Poetry whistled an exclamation that said he was getting excited. It also seemed to say that he really believed me.

No wonder Mother Addie had been acting so strange. She'd lost one of her little red-haired family and, like Little Bo Peep's lost sheep, didn't know where to find it. It would never come home waggling its pretty little curly tail behind it. It would never go to market, never have roast beef, and never go, "Wee-wee-wee" all the way home.

Just then we heard an excited running boy's voice calling from the woods across the road, using the high-pitched tone anybody uses when he is calling a horse.

I unlatched my eyes from the chocolate-colored stains on the ground near the pigpen gate and looked past THEODORE COLLINS on our mailbox across the graveled road to the woods. I saw a blue-jeaned, striped-tee-shirted boy with flushed face, mussed-up hair, crooked nose, and dragonfly-like eyes spindle-legging his way in the path made by barefoot boys toward the fence and us.

"You guys seen anything of Old Molly?" he

yelled, and kept on running—and also yelling up and all around, "Co, Molly. Co, Molly! Where in the world are you?"

Molly, I knew, was their sorrel mare who was always getting out of their pasture and into other people's pastures or woods or cornfields and was almost as wild as Shorty Long's blue cow you read all about in the story, *Blue Cow at Sugar Creek*.

Even though Poetry and I had something extra serious on our minds, he managed to say mischievously, "Leave her alone and she'll come home, bringing her tail behind her."

"She'll bring *two* tails if she does come," Dragonfly panted, still short of breath from running.

"Two tails?" Poetry squawked back. "Don't be funny!"

"She's going to have a little colt," Dragonfly explained excitedly. "She's run away somewhere so she can have it all by herself. Come on, you guys! Help me find her! I saw her tracks down at the spring, but she wasn't there. She might be along the bayou somewhere!"

I don't know why I said what I said right then —and maybe shouldn't have, 'cause it almost scared Dragonfly out of what few wits he had. Even though I said it to Poetry and not to Dragonfly, the worried little guy overheard it. It was:

"Wildcats would rather eat colt meat than any other kind, except deer and little pigs."

Dragonfly's answer was a scared scream: "Wildcats!"

There wasn't any use to try to keep the pop-eyed little guy in the dark about what we knew. So as fast as we could, we told him about yesterday and last night, showed him the dried blood at Addie's gate, let him count the pigs, and got him as scared as we could before reminding him of what most hunters know, that a wildcat doesn't ever attack a human being unless it's cornered or thinks it is and also thinks it *has* to attack to protect itself.

"But I thought Old Stubtail was in Parke County!" Dragonfly said.

"He was *supposed* to be. But maybe he had a brother," I answered, and was surprised at what I had just thought of to say.

The three of us made a quick decision to get going on the search for Old Molly, to get her home and safe in her box stall, so she could celebrate the birth of her baby colt in peace and where there wouldn't be any danger of Old Stubtail sneaking up on her wherever she was and killing and eating her colt.

I was a little bothered about the last part of the eighth commandment for hunting safety when I went into the house to get Betty Lizzie. That commandment seemed to be staring at me from the examination paper I'd written out for Dad: "Don't hunt with more than one companion."

I told Poetry about it, and he said, kind of lofty-like, "Oh that's when they have a gun apiece! Don't you remember? Sometimes the whole gang of us has gone hunting at night with Circus' dad."

I wasn't sure he was right, so I ordered both Dragonfly and Poetry to stay behind me as we started toward the spring and the bayou to see if we could find Dragonfly's family's sorrel mare.

At the spring we saw her tracks but of course she herself wasn't there.

Up the hill we went, past the leaning linden tree, past the black widow stump and east along the border of the bayou to the rail fence, on the other side of which is Dragonfly's dad's pasture I was in the lead with Betty Lizzie, ready to shoot if I had to.

At the fence a covey of quail exploded out of their hiding place and fanned out into the air in seven or eight different directions, like a giant-sized peacock tail opening. They skimmed over the fence and across a corner of the field and disappeared in good quail cover about a hundred yards up the bayou.

I had Betty Lizzie up and pointed. I almost

pulled the trigger but didn't 'cause I knew I'd just waste a shot. Besides, the season wasn't open and if I killed a quail I'd be breaking the law.

I kept Betty Lizzie's safety on all the time, which is part of rule number four, and unloaded her before climbing over the fence to go down into the marshy sedge and brush that bordered the bayou pond.

Over the fence with Betty Lizzie loaded again, I was careful to keep her muzzle always pointed away from all of us—either up or down—so if I stumbled over anything and she was discharged, the bullet would go off toward the sky or into the ground.

We hadn't any sooner reached the bayou pond and started to skirt it than Dragonfly let out a yell. "There she is! Away over there by the swimming hole! See her! She's all right and safe!"

She was safe, all right, but she wasn't all right— not in her mind. She acted like she didn't have good horse sense but was nervous and trembling like Old Red Addie had been.

Dragonfly let out another yell then, broke out from behind me and started on a knee-pumping sprint toward the swimming hole and Old Molly, crying, "Look! She's not fat anymore. She's already had her colt! Let's go see what color it is!"

I quick swung Betty's muzzle away, and as quick

unloaded her on account of it wasn't safe to have a loaded gun around such an excited boy.

He got there ahead of either Poetry or me. "Look," he exclaimed proudly, pointing to Molly's colt, lying on its side on the ground, "He's got a white spot on his forehead and one on his rump and—and—"

Then that spindle-legged, pop-eyed, crooked-nosed, excited little guy let out a blood-curdling scream, crying, *"He's dead! He's been killed! He's got blood all over him!"*

7

It was one of the saddest sights I ever saw: Molly's beautiful brand-new colt with a long snow-white streak down its forehead all the way from its forelock to the tip of its nose, a white spot on its right rump—lying a few feet from the creek, dead.

I felt myself cringing and scared and wondering. I could see where the teeth of some wild animal had fanged the colt's neck in front of the shoulders and had broken it. And just *behind* the shoulders, there was a bloody place where something had eaten its way in, dug out the heart and liver.

"My colt!" Dragonfly sobbed. "Dad was going to give it to me! What coulda done it! What coulda!" He broke into a wild kind of sobbing that was like a knife jabbing into my heart. Already the bluebottle flies were swarming around the dead colt.

I was holding onto Betty Lizzie, feeling safer by having her with us—and all the time I was wondering where Old Stubtail was by now. What if right that very minute he would break out from behind the shrubbery to get a middle-of-the-morning snack!

It was a shame to have such a beautiful morning spoiled by such dangerous excitement. I was so stirred up inside that the water singing in the Sugar Creek riffle below the swimming hole, the friendly breeze fanning my face, and the juicy notes of the red-winged blackbirds in the trees that bordered the bayou, didn't seem wonderful at all, like they nearly always had other times when I was there.

Dragonfly was so angry and excited and unhappy that I decided to try to cheer him up a little by saying, "We'll put Circus' dad's hounds on his trail again, and this time we'll get him. We'll—"

Dragonfly didn't let me finish. He cut in excitedly with his voice trembling and with fire in his eyes, exclaiming, "We'll catch him and kill him and cut his heart out!"

It had been a long time since I'd seen that little crooked-nosed boy so angry· If he hadn't been a Christian he'd probably have used swear words—which not a one of the gang ever used. It wouldn't be fair to the Person we all tried to live for and whose Name shouldn't be treated like it was just so much dirt.

I'd maybe better explain right here that it was our lady Sunday school teacher who had taught us that, saying one Sunday morning in class, "Cowards and thoughtless people throw the Name of our Saviour around like it was just so much dirt."

It was bad enough having one little red-haired pig stolen and probably eaten. It seemed worse for Old Molly to have her only colt killed right in front of her eyes maybe not more than a few hours after it had been born. It had hardly learned to walk.

Right then is when we heard a dog's voice, a long-toned, bell-like tremolo that I knew in a flash belonged to Ichabod Brown.

"It's Ichabod!" Dragonfly exclaimed. "He's already found the trail! Come on!" He started off on the run in the path that led to the bayou with Poetry and me right after him.

I had Betty Lizzie still unloaded, wondering how I could obey all the Ten Commandments of Hunting Safety when there were three of us and when it'd be almost impossible to keep the fifth commandment which was never to climb a tree or a fence with a loaded gun. We'd probably have a fence to climb every few minutes. If Ichabod had really found Old Stubtail's trail, he might—this time—actually stay with it and we might all of a sudden come upon the colt killer at bay against a rock wall or an outcropping in Old Man Paddler's hills, and I might have to shoot quick or one or the other of us would get killed.

It seemed like I *ought* to have the gun loaded. It also seemed like I ought not.

I knew what Dad would say if he were there. Also what Big Jim, our leader, would order us *not* to do: not to let ourselves get into a dangerous hurry but to call Ichabod off the trail, wait for Circus' dad to get back from Parke County with his hounds, and organize a hunt with grown-up men.

I kept Betty Lizzie unloaded, though, so it would be safe for Poetry and me to run pell-mell after Dragonfly and also after Ichabod whose voice said he was on the other side of the bayou up in the woods near where we'd flushed the covey of quail.

Pretty soon we were there ourselves. But Ichabod was already gone, galloping in the direction of the leaning linden tree, following the row of evergreens toward the black widow stump. And Dragonfly was still running faster than either Poetry or I.

I yelled for him to stop and he wouldn't. I was close enough to him to see that he had his boy scout knife out and its blade open. That *really* made me worry.

"Stop!" I ordered him in my most savage voice, "Don't ever run with an open-bladed knife! You could fall on it and kill yourself! You could cut your *own* heart out!"

It seemed I had already warned him too late, because all of a sudden that spindle-legged little guy, who had just reached the incline above the spring, stumbled over something and went down in a topsy-turvy flipflopping fall. He had been running so fast that falling didn't stop him. He rolled over the lip of the hill and disappeared.

I screamed and ran faster, expecting that when I got there I'd see he had hurt himself with his own knife.

Then, from the direction of the papaw bushes I heard Circus' voice scolding loud and hard, "Stop it! Come back here, you mongrel! Leave that rabbit alone!"

I knew Ichabod wasn't any mongrel, which is a dog of mixed breed, but was a purebred black and tan. Circus was calling him a mongrel because he was disgusted with him.

In only a few jiffies Poetry and I were where Dragonfly had fallen. I certainly felt relieved when I saw he hadn't cut himself in the fall but was only sprawled in the puddle on the other side of the spring reservoir, his knife lying beside him, both hands covered with mud—and his face, jeans, and shirt.

Circus didn't seem to realize what was going on nor that we were anywhere around. He kept on calling Ichabod in a scolding voice. I noticed also that he had picked up a switch and was waiting for his hound to come to him so he could give him a lesson in hunting—not to get off onto a rabbit trail when he was supposed to be on a red-hot other animal trail.

Just like I thought he was going to do, Circus sure enough gave his cute, very sad little hound a small switching and scolding, saying down to him —still not realizing we were around—"Rabbits are *trash!* Do you understand? I started you off on a coon trail and you were doing fine until that bunny jumped up right in front of your nose, and you let him interrupt you! If you're going to be a trash-trailer, you'll be a terrible disappointment. You won't be worth a hill of beans if you don't learn to concentrate!"

I broke in then, saying, "Rabbits aren't trash!" I was thinking how very cute small bunnies really are and also remembering one I had seen being eaten by a huge stub-tailed wildcat down by the mouth of the branch yesterday.

"*Part* of the time, they're trash," Circus answered like a teacher correcting a boy in class. "Any game the hunter isn't after at the time is *trash*. That's the name they give it. I'm trying to train Ichabod not to get sidetracked onto anything—rabbit, possum, skunk—*anything*—when I've started him on something else."

I looked down at little Ichabod's sad face and felt sorry for him. It seemed a shame he had had to be punished. I guess maybe Circus felt even worse than I did about it 'cause a second later he was down on his knees hugging his cute little black and tan dog and crooning to him, "I've got a plan for your life. I can't let you be a trash-killer. You'll never be any good at trailing wildcats like your mother if you don't learn now! Understand?"

Dragonfly, who was up and washing his hands and face at the spring, heard what Circus had just said, and called up the incline, "Old Stubtail's come back and he's killed Molly's new colt and—"

Our spindle-legged little friend came storming up, his open knife in his now-clean right hand, his clothes still mud-spattered, his hair mussed up but with a set face. "Let's put Ichabod on his trail and chase him down and kill him!"

In only a little while Circus, Poetry, Ichabod, Dragonfly, and I were back at the swimming hole looking at the dead colt, studying its claw-raked sides and the place in front of the shoulders where powerful fangs had broken its neck and at the red

81

hole *behind* the shoulders where the heart and liver had been dug out and eaten.

Circus stood with narrowed eyes, looking down. There was excitement going on in his mind. I noticed his fists were doubled up and his jaw muscles tensing and untensing.

Something exciting was going on in Ichabod's nose too. He hadn't any sooner smelled the colt than he started running in a circle all around us and along the creek bank like he was trying to find something he had lost—or else his nose was smelling something he'd never smelled before. Whatever it was was setting him crazy.

Suddenly that cute little black and tan dog lifted his long-nosed head and let loose a wild, shrill call with a bell-like tremolo in it like a scared ghost calling for help, and took off in a long-legged excited gallop toward the bayou.

"He's found the trail!" Circus cried. The tone of his voice sent a hunter's thrill chasing up and down my spine. In a whirlwind of a jiffy we were all following as fast as we could run.

Across the narrow strip of Dragonfly's dad's cornfield to the bayou and the neck of dry ground between the two long ponds, up the incline to the rail fence and the border of evergreens, the cute little hound went, with the four of us close behind.

At the rail fence the trail swung south along the

82

hedgerow toward Bumblebee Hill and the cemetery at the top, through the cemetery and on and
on and still on, following the thicket that skirted
the rock wall which, Circus said, was good "cat
cover."

And now Ichabod was making a beeline for the
Theodore Collins' family house. At the elderberry
bushes across the road from the walnut tree and
our mailbox the pup began to whimper and to act
worried like he had lost the trail. But only for a
few seconds. In a flash he was over the fence and
across the graveled road to our front gate, running
from one end to the other to find a place to get
over or through.

That's when we heard the sound of a car and
saw a cloud of dust up the road. It was Dad coming back from Memory City. Boy oh boy, would
we ever have something to tell him! That Old
Stubtail was back in our territory again and had
killed one of our little pigs, eaten a rabbit at the
mouth of the branch, and killed Molly Gilbert's
new baby colt and she hadn't even had a chance
to celebrate its birth!

I was wondering what kind of a new cousin I
had at Memory City—a boy or a girl—and how
Wally and his nonsensical dog were.

I swung open the gate to let Dad in. Ichabod
didn't even bother to try to find out who was com-

ing. Only one thing seemed important to him. He raced through the gate, his nose to the ground, let out another long, piercing tremolo, shot across the lawn, past the plum tree and the iron pitcher pump straight for Addie's house and lot.

Dad swung the car in and stopped in a cloud of dust. The back door of the car was thrust open and what to my wondering eyes should tumble out but a red-haired, freckled-faced boy my size and an excited copper-colored dog that you already know too much about if you've read the story *10,000 Minutes at Sugar Creek*.

Dad had brought home with him from Memory City my set-minded, hard-to-get-along-with city cousin, Walford Sensenbrenner, and his uncontrollable dog, Alexander the Coppersmith!

Why on earth had Dad done a thing like that to me and to the Sugar Creek Gang!

What and why and how on earth would we ever manage to live for as long as Alexander the Coppersmith and his master stayed with us?

They certainly had arrived at an exciting time— and at a dangerous one too. Just *how* dangerous, none of us knew. Not even Ichabod who was already out by Addie's gate running in a worried circle like he had lost the trail again.

8

ALEXANDER the Coppersmith had come again!

In a flurry of fleeting flashes I remembered the wild ten thousand minutes we had had that other summer—especially the one exciting, nerve-tingling adventure I'd never be able to forget as long as I lived.

Honestly, that mongrel of a city-bred dog wasn't afraid of the most dangerous danger there ever was! He had even tackled headfirst a snorting, blindly mad, long-horned shorthorn bull, actually sinking his sharp teeth into the bull's nose, holding on for dear life. The worried, stormy-minded, wild-eyed long-horned shorthorn bull, trying to get Alexander the Coppersmith to let go, had swung his body around and with a mighty bellow and shake of his head had tossed that copper-colored dog toward the sky.

Alexander, like a streak of reddish brown, went sailing through the air with the greatest of ease like the man on the flying trapeze.

But that's the other story. Right now I have to tell you about the savage, pig-stealing, colt-killing wildcat which right that very second Circus' new black and tan hound pup was trailing out near Old Red Addie's gate—one of whose piggies would never again lie in the straw with its mother.

Ichabod seemed to have only one thing on his mind. He didn't even notice Alexander the Coppersmith but was following his snuffling nose all around the gate where I knew there was chocolate-colored pig's blood and where last night I had seen two green eyes reflecting light from my flashlight and a grayish, brownish shadow slinking along the garden fence toward the twin pignut trees and the orchard below them.

Right that second Alexander was standing straight-nosed and stiff-legged in the direction of the gate where Ichabod was worrying his way through a tangle of cross-scents, trying to decide which direction Old Stubtail had gone.

To make things more interesting and noisy, Mixy who had been lazying on our sloping, outside cellar door, woke out of her middle-of-the-morning nap and came as far as the boardwalk to see what kind of animal had just come plopping out of the car with my city cousin, Wally.

She was probably recalling the very fast time Alexander had come to our house: the Thanksgiving Day when he had been leading one of our turkeys around by the neck, one end of the rope tied to Alexander's collar and the other to the turkey's neck. Seeing Mixy for the first time, Alex had leaped into fast dog life and chased her wildly across the barnyard with the tied turkey tumbling after.

Or, Mixy might be remembering other fights she had had with different neighborhood dogs. Anyway, all of a sudden, Alexander spied her and moved stiff-legged toward her while she stood stiff-backed and bristling, eyeing him back. In a second now, I thought, there would be action.

And there was. A copper-colored city dog made a copper-colored head-and-teeth-first dash at a country cat.

Mixy crouched, flattened her ears, and stood her ground. The very second Alexander got to where she was, she thrust out a fierce, fast right front foot with sharp talons on it and slashed and slashed and slashed again, letting loose a jumble of yowls and hisses and wild meows all mixed up with Alexander the Coppersmith's gruff, excited, angry barks and yelps.

The fight was so fierce, so fast, you couldn't tell which of the two animals belonged to the cat family and which to the dog.

Dad, Dragonfly, Circus, Poetry, and I were in

87

the fight too—with our voices, that is. Wally was yelling, "Sic'em!" And the rest of us were rooting for Mixy—all except Dad who was ordering them both to stop.

I was proud of Mixy, the way she stayed right in the middle of that hissing, spitting, yowling tooth-and-claw, cat-and-dog fight. All of a sudden, though, she must have decided she had had enough—or had *done* enough to her enemy 'cause, as quick as scat that cat turned herself into a streak of black and white lightning shooting across the barnyard to the barn, to the hole just below the window where she would be safe—if she got there first.

She *did* get there first and was safe, and I was proud of her that she knew when to quit and run away. She'd live to fight another day.

I expected Wally's mongrel to stay at the small hole into which Mixy had disappeared and bark and bark and bark and pant and try to squeeze himself in after her, but he didn't. Instead, he gave several gruff disgusted halfhearted barks in Mixy's direction, swung his copper-colored body around, and came trotting back toward the iron pitcher pump where we all were, his tongue hanging out, his sides heaving a little with panting, and with a proud grin on his face that seemed to say, "There! I saved all your lives! I just licked the fur off a savage black and white cat that might have killed all of you if I hadn't! I drove her into a hole under the barn and she's scared to even stick her nose out!"

The expression on his proud face was the same kind he gets when he chases a car down the road.

Just that second from near the pignut trees, I heard a shrill, long-toned tremolo and it was Ichabod's dog-voice crying, "Come on, you, and help me! While you've been wasting your time on a worthless house cat, I've been untangling the trail of a pig-stealing, colt-killing *wild*cat!"

"Whooooooooo . . . . . who . . . . . whooooooooo . . . . ."

Say, when Circus' cute little hound let loose that long-toned, high-pitched tremolo from the twin pignut trees where he was at the time, it brought all of us to excited life.

"He's found the trail again," Circus cried, and away he started on a fast gallop past the toolshed and the chicken house on his way to catch up with his excited black and tan pup which already was halfway to the orchard fence.

Alexander the Coppersmith had come to even more excited life than the rest of us. The very second he heard Ichabod's wailing tremolo he took one quick stiff-legged, straight-nosed look toward the galloping hound with an expression on his face

89

that seemed to say that up to now he hadn't even noticed there was another dog around. He'd been so busy saving our lives. Then, just as if Ichabod's excited bawling was a stick somebody had thrown into a creek and he was expected to swim out and get it and bring it back, he was off in a copper streak of speed to join in the fun or whatever it was that was going on.

"Attaboy!" Wally cried to his mongrel. "Go get him!"

At the orchard fence where there was a lot of grass and weeds and wild raspberry bushes which was good cover for quail and which nearly always, in the winter especially, was a shelter for rabbits, Ichabod ran into trail trouble again. I could tell by the way he was acting he was trying to decide whether the wildcat had gone through the fence or had followed the fence row to Poetry's dad's woods in the direction of the mouth of the branch where, yesterday, I'd seen his fierce face for the first time.

Any second now, Alexander the Coppersmith would get to where Ichabod was circling and zig-zagging all around trying to find what he had lost, and *then* what would happen!

I let out a yell for him to stop, to come back, 'cause I knew he didn't have the least idea what a wildcat smelled like or how to follow a cold scent forward or backward. Not knowing how serious things were—a stolen pig, three lambs killed on Harm Groenwald's farm, a brand-new baby colt lying by the swimming hole with its heart and liver eaten out—he'd probably think Ichabod's bawling and strange circlings and zigzaggings were some kind of a game which country dogs play.

In a few jiffies he was there and all over every-where, getting in Ichabod's way, biting at him playfully, and barking as if what few wits he had had turned into a Sugar Creek cyclone.

He was also like a car that didn't have good brakes 'cause in a fast charge at Ichabod he whammed into his shoulder with his own shoulder and bowled him over and the two of them landed in a tangled-up scramble scratchety-sizzle in the raspberry bushes. And that's when Ichabod's voice changed into a series of short, sharp, more-than-ever-excited barks. For a second I thought he had lost his temper and there was going to be a fierce, fast dogfight there in the bushes.

But I was wrong. Instead, all in a brown flash a bunny shot out into the open and raced hippety-fast-hop down the fence row toward Poetry's dad's woods, with Ichabod and Alexander giving chase with a two-voiced bedlam of dog voices, which was enough to scare the poor rabbit even worse than Peter Rabbit had been scared in the story in our school reader when Mr. McGregor was after him with a garden rake.

Seeing the rabbit flying in long leaps ahead of the also-flying, excited, barking dogs, Circus let out a yell, "Hey, Ichabod! Stop! That's a *rabbit!* Come back here!"

To the rest of us he complained, "He's going to be hard to teach! I'll have to give him another switching!"

With that he quick stooped, picked up a branch Dad had pruned from the peach tree by the fence, and was off on a fast run toward the other fence away down at the end of our pasture. Both dogs were running excitedly back and forth trying to find a place where they could get through or over the fence. The smart bunny had already squeezed through and was safe somewhere in Poetry's dad's woods.

Both dogs heard Circus' angry voice, and both dogs started back toward where we were. I felt sorry for little Ichabod 'cause the biography of my half-long life had had maybe a dozen kinds of switches mixed up in it. And if there is anything that hurts me worse than getting a licking myself, it's to see somebody's pet get switched or even scolded—a hound especially, on account of he always acts so sad, and crouches very low and looks up at you with every wrinkle on its long nosed face seeming to say, "Please, Mister. I'm sorry. I didn't know it was wrong to do it. Please . . . !"

The closer Ichabod got to Circus, the sadder he looked, and by the time he was within ten feet, he was actually crawling. Then he stopped, looked up with the saddest brown eyes you ever saw, every movement saying, "I'm sorry . . . please . . .!"

I took one look at Circus' set face and knew he was thinking hard and wishing he didn't have to do what I also knew he had to do. Nobody could train a hound *not* to hunt rabbits, or to get side-tracked, unless the hound knew for sure his master wouldn't stand for it.

I hadn't known Little Jim, the littlest member of the gang, was anywhere around until all of a sudden from behind us I heard his tearful voice almost screaming, "Don't! Don't Circus. Don't! He doesn't know any better. He. . . ."

"That's why I'm punishing him," Circus called back grimly, "so he *will* know."

Then Circus said something I didn't understand at the time, but which later, I did. He looked around at all of us with kind of sad eyes first. "I'm giving him a licking not to punish him for being *bad* but to make him a good trailer. I have a good

93

plan for his life and I have to help him find out what it is."

The switching Circus gave his cute little black and tan hound pup was about the easiest switching a dog ever got. With one hand he held onto Ichabod's collar, and with the other he swung the switch . . . one . . . two . . . three . . . four. The strokes weren't even half or one fourth as hard as the last six or seven my father had given his son that very summer. Circus switched Ichabod harder with his voice, saying crossly, "Rabbits are *out!* Do you understand? Out! When you're on a coon trail—or a fox or a wildcat—you're not to let yourself get sidetracked! Understand!"

Then all of a sudden Circus flung his switch to the ground, dropped to his knees, pressed his cheek against his hound's head, hugged him close, and begged, "I'm sorry, pal! Please don't hate me for it! But I *had* to do it. Even if it was bad company that got you started. Bad company, do you hear! Don't ever let any other dog lead you astray!" Circus looked away then, and I noticed he was glaring angrily at a fidgety Alexander the Coppersmith not more than ten feet away.

Wally overheard that and exclaimed, "Don't you *dare* call my dog bad company! He's a good dog!"

I noticed there were tears in Circus' eyes like there had been in his voice when he had apologized to Ichabod. Say, you never saw a dog change his attitude so quickly. All in a second he was happy again, nuzzling his face up to Circus' and wagging his long tail. Everybody was forgiven to everybody.

For some reason, it seemed like Ichabod was trying to say to Circus, "Don't feel bad. I'll forgive you . . . !"

I couldn't help thinking about Alexander, wondering if anybody had a good plan for *his* life, if his life would ever be worth anything. I'd tried so hard to teach him a few dog manners the other summer when Wally had come to spend 10,000 minutes at our house.

There certainly was a difference in the way those two canines were getting trained, also in the way they came back from chasing the rabbit. Ichabod had come back to his master with a sad face, acting sorry for what he had done, whatever it was. Wally's mongrel had come racing back proudly, his long tongue hanging out, a grin on his whiskered face that almost screamed at us as if to say: "There! I chased *another* wild animal away, clear down to the woods. I've saved all your lives again!"

Wally, seeing what Circus had done, must have thought he ought to give Alex a little training too. He quick picked up the switch Circus had tossed away and started after him, scolding and saying, "Come here, you rascal! Rabbits are out. . . . Understand? Out!"

But there wasn't any change in the attitude of Alexander the Coppersmith. Instead of coming humbly to his master to find out what he'd done that he shouldn't have, he stopped stock-still, stood stiff-legged and straight-nosed, gave two or three short gruff, disgusted barks, tossed his head, whirled all the way around, and ran off toward the pignut trees. There he stopped and looked back.

"Come here, you rabbit chaser!" Wally yelled crossly, and with the switch in his hand started on the run toward him.

It was a very interesting sight to watch—Alexander the Coppersmith standing stiff-legged, looking down the incline at us, his beady eyes on Wally and the switch and Wally, red-haired and freckled and flushed faced, hurrying toward him, shouting, "Don't you dare run away! Do you hear me? Don't you *dare!*"

But his mongrel dared. He whirled his body about, looked in our direction again and bounded away with Wally right after him.

"Wait!" Circus called to Wally. "I'll get him for you." He quickly stooped, picked up an old stick of some kind, yelled a cheerful yell toward the pignut trees, tossed the two-foot-long stick as far as he could in the direction of the orchard fence where the raspberry bushes were, calling at the same time, "Go get it!"

That was a game Alex understood. We'd played it with him many a time the week he'd spent here last year. Every time we had tossed a stick anywhere, even out into the water, he'd raced after it, caught it up in his happy mouth, and come flying back to us.

There was a copper streak of dog shooting across the stretch of pasture, and in less than a jiffy or two Alex was back where we were. "Don't you touch him with that switch!" Circus ordered Wally. "It's been too long since he chased the rabbit. He wouldn't understand anything you'd do to him now. Besides you might *want* him to chase rabbits. A good rabbit dog is worth money."

And that was that.

Dad called from the gate near Addie's apartment house, "You boys seen anything of a missing pig? One of the pigs is missing!"

I'd almost forgotten Dad, my mind being so tangled up with everything else.

In a little while we were where he was, showing him the chocolate-colored dried blood and telling him about Dragonfly's dead colt down by the swimming hole, the savage-faced wildcat I'd seen eating a bunny yesterday when I'd been fishing at the mouth of the branch, and the excitement of last night at the chicken house.

I could see Dad's jaw muscles tensing and knew he was getting stirred up inside. We were really in a situation—with Circus' dad gone to Parke County with his hounds to help the farmers over there catch the sheep-killing predator, and all of a sudden to find out Old Stubtail was back in our own territory again, killing right and left. Something'd have to be done. We'd have to get a phone call through to Dan Brown as quick as we could and get him back here with the dogs.

Dad got his thoughts interrupted right then by the sound of a long, high-pitched tremolo from down near the raspberry bushes. It was Ichabod Brown again. He was zigzagging all around where he and Alexander the Coppersmith had had their tangled-up scramble and where the rabbit, which had been born and bred in the brier patch, had had his nest and out of which he had exploded like a grayish-brown rocket and gone hippety-fast-hop down the fence row.

Ichabod was making such a noisy noise and seemed so extra excited that I guessed he had found Old Stubtail's trail again and was untangling it.

Wally had a different idea 'cause as soon as he'd heard Ichabod's tremolo, he said to Circus, "Lot of good it did to give him a lickin'! There he goes again on another rabbit."

But there Ichabod *didn't* go—not on another rabbit, anyway. He whisked through an opening in the fence and was off in a long-voiced gallop right down through the center of the orchard, his nose to the ground every few feet, his musical tremolo singing out on the warm sunshiny air every few seconds.

"Come on!" different ones of us yelled to the rest of us. "Let's follow him!"

Dad stopped us all right then with his gruff voice ordering, "Wait, boys. A wildcat would tear your hound to shreds if he brought him to bay. Call off your dog, Circus!"

Circus had a different idea. "But the trail's hot! It's fresh! The time to chase him to his den is *now!* It might be a week before we'd run onto another hot track like this one."

Dad wasn't used to having a boy anywhere near my age talk back to him, so he used a very strong dad-like voice when he ordered Circus, "Call him off! You don't want your hound killed! I'll go in and get your father on the phone right away and tell him Old Stubtail's back here, and to come on home fast."

I could see Circus didn't want to obey any other

boy's father, but he did try to by calling Ichabod and whistling for him.

Ichabod also had a different idea. Already his excitement was away down at the other end of the orchard. I could see him at the woven wire fence down there, squeezing through into Poetry's dad's woods.

"We've got to stop him!" Circus said grimly. I could tell from the expression on his face that he believed Dad, that it'd never do to let an innocent hound pup get into a fierce, fast fang-fight with a wildcat. Ichabod would be torn to pieces. The teeth I'd seen on Old Stubtail yesterday were big enough, sharp enough, and strong enough to bite right through a dog's head—a dog the size of Ichabod.

All of us except Alexander the Coppersmith started on the run after Circus to try to help him stop his hound from getting killed. The only reason Alexander *didn't* start was that already he was down where Ichabod was and was running wild all around in front of and behind and in the way of Ichabod, like he was trying to get attention or he wanted to make us think it was his own nonsensical nose that was doing all the trailing. I knew that copper-colored excitable city dog didn't have the least idea what was going on.

What I didn't know was that sooner even than

a half hour Alexander the Coppersmith was going to see his first wildcat and find out that chasing a black and white house cat into a hole under a barn, was a lot different from all of a sudden happening onto a tufted-eared, twenty-eight toothed, sharp-taloned, savage-tempered *really* wild wildcat.

9

Say, Ichabod Brown was one of the fastest trailers that ever trailed a trail. He was also, I thought, one of the most stubborn hound pups I ever saw or heard.

In my mind, while we were running pell-mell after him and Alexander the Coppersmith, I had one main purpose—to stop Ichabod from all of a sudden catching up with Old Stubtail and getting his eyes scratched out.

One thing I *didn't* realize at first was that with all the yelling Circus was doing, ordering his pup to stop, he wasn't using a scolding voice. He was yelling "Stop! Leave that wildcat alone! You'll get your ears slit to ribbons! You're no good as a catch dog! You're only a trailer!" But he *wasn't* using a tone of voice like the tone he had used several times that morning when he'd been disgusted with Ichy for trailing trash.

It sounded more like Dan Brown's son was whooping it up at a basketball game, rooting for

102

his team to win, like he was urging his cute little black and tan purebred hound pup to stay on the job. To keep on keeping on. To chase Old Stubtail to his lair or actually catch up with him and get into a fierce, fast fang-fight with him or something.

When we reached the mouth of the branch where I'd first seen Old Stubtail eating a rabbit and where I'd had the dream of wildcats riding up and down a golden-staired escalator, I panted to Circus, "How come he won't obey you! How come he keeps right on?"

He leaped across a narrow place in the stream, landed on the other side, and answered me, "He's not trailing trash! If I'd scold him now, he might think we didn't *want* him to trail wildcats! He'd think *I* think he was trailing trash—and he might be spoiled! I gotta let him do it!"

"But my father ordered you to stop him!" I protested.

Wally and the rest of the gang were quite a ways behind us, and only *I* heard what Circus answered. "Your father? *My* father would want me to whoop it up for Ichabod! He'd let him learn to trail—then right at the last minute, if there was any danger, he'd use a different tone of voice. He'd stop him from *catching* but not from *trailing!*"

And that was that. I realized that Dad himself was back at the house trying to put through a

103

long-distance call to Dan Brown in Parke County somewhere—and here *we* were—already a half mile from home, and he couldn't even order his own son to stop. Dad hadn't noticed that I had Betty Lizzie with me, and of course he hadn't ordered me not to take her.

Now that the chase was on, we might run into an emergency that'd mean I either had to use Betty Lizzie or one or the other of six boys and two dogs might get killed.

Pound . . . pound . . . pound . . . pound. My heart was beating hard, and it wasn't just from running.

All of a sudden from behind me I heard Little Jim's cute little excited voice exclaim, "Hey, everybody! Look—out there in the creek!"

I looked, and there, straight out from the willow where I'd had my whopper of a bass on the stringer, was a V-shaped water trail moving parallel with the shore with the small brown head of some wild animal at the apex of it. A glad feeling shot through me. There was proof that I had had a fish on the stringer. I didn't answer Little Jim but I did yell to Poetry, "There, Smarty-fat, there's what ate my whopper of a bass!"

Poetry was closer to me than I thought, and his answer was so loud in my ears it almost deafened me. "Right, Smarty-thin! I knew it all the time. I saw that muskrat yesterday while I was up on the tree trunk."

On and on and still on we went. At the cave Ichabod, with Alexander running circles all around him and acting like he was enjoying the new country dog game, didn't even bother to take one tiny sniff but zigzagged right on following the path into the swamp, just like Jay and Bawler had done quite a few other times when they'd been on Old Stubtail's trail. Boy, oh boy, oh boy!

"He's headed for Old Man Paddler's hills again!" Dragonfly's raspy voice cried from behind all of us. He was short of breath on account of hay fever and a little asthma.

I wasn't quite sure I was doing right, but it seemed like I was. I knew my father didn't want us to do what we were doing—that is, he did want Circus to call off his dog—and he would also expect his son to help Circus do it.

Yet, my same father was always happy when the gang was together having what he and Mom called "wholesome fun" if we weren't supposed to be doing something else at the time. The only thing was, he *didn't* know that while Dan Brown's son was ordering his dog to stop, he was using a tone of voice that was like saying, "Atta boy, Ichabod! Keep on doing what you're doing. You're doing a swell job. Go to it! You're a swell dog. Wonderful!"

We had to slow down in the swamp because Ichabod was having nose trouble, not being able to untangle the wildcat's pretty-smart, mixed-up trail.

In a few minutes now we'd get to the middle of the swamp where the water, backing into it from Sugar Creek, had made a big pond. I was remembering another time when Wally and Alexander had been with us and Wally'd kept his nervous quadruped on a leash. We hadn't wanted to run the risk of his running wild all over everywhere. He might accidentally get out into the quagmire, sink down, and never come back up.

It was such an exciting place, with marsh hens swimming along, leaving nervous V-shaped water trails behind them, turtles which had been sunning themselves on a log, all of a sudden plopping off into the water, dragonflies sailing around all over, redwing blackbirds furnishing the music. The whole area was a happy place to be, to feel lazy in. The grassy hillock on the shore begged a drowsy boy to take an afternoon nap.

Ichabod wasn't bothered by marsh hens swimming, redwings singing, turtles splashing, or anything. He was on a trail of something that wasn't

106

trash. His master was whooping it up for him to keep on keeping on. So he kept on.

It was different with Alexander the Copper-smith. He, when we got to the edge of the pond, stopped still and stood stiff-legged and straight-nosed in the direction of the middle of the swamp like he was using his mind for something that wasn't play. If he *was* thinking, I knew what was bothering him. It was the memory of that other time when we'd brought him through and he'd had the fierce, fast, underwater fight with a snapping turtle.

I looked to see what was worrying him, and, sure enough, there was a giant-sized turtle, his nose and heavy-lidded eyes looking like drops of transparent blood sticking up just above the surface of the water. I got a glimpse of the rest of him *under* the water just as I had the first time I'd seen him, and he was even bigger than he'd been then, having had time to grow some more.

Alexander wasn't interested in getting out into the water to see what was there. Dragonfly, re-membering that the other time somebody had thrown a stick out into the water and Alex had plunged in after it—and that was when he'd gotten into the battle with the snapper—I say, Dragonfly right that second tossed a piece of driftwood out toward the snapper's nose. Alex let out a whimper and made a dive for Wally, who, the second he got to him, quick grabbed his collar and snapped on his leash.

Alexander, might not have good sense most of the time, but he did know enough to know it is better to use your head than it is to get it snapped off by a giant-sized snapper. Or as Dad says, "It's better to have good sense than it is to be brave."

Well, it wasn't any time to enjoy our favorite nature's paradise. Certainly not right then. From what seemed like maybe two hundred yards away, there came the high-pitched musical wail of Ichabod's tremolo. He'd untangled Stubtail's trail and was running in full cry in the direction of the rocky hills above Old Man Paddler's cabin.

Circus let out a thrilling yell, crying, "He's headed for the Haunted House! I'll bet Old Stubtail's got his den in the attic where the old mother coon used to live!"

And the chase was on again.

What would happen this time? Would it be like all the other times when Dan Brown's hounds had run red hot on Stubtail's trail, up and down the hills, across dry canyons, in and out of brier thickets, along the edges of outcroppings and high ledges with jagged rocks below, and then finally had lost the scent and couldn't find it again? I wished with my whole heart it'd be different.

We hadn't any sooner reached the clearing on the other side of the swamp than Wally's dog changed from a scaredy-cat to an excited copper-colored, wild-running, impossible-to-manage mongrel again.

"Oh no, you don't," Wally cried to him, holding onto his leash with all his strength. "You're not going to run wild up there in those rocks! You don't watch your footing! You'd make a dash for a rabbit or a bird or leap across a chasm and miss the other side, and down you'd go. Stop!" He screamed his order toward the animal on the other end of his leash.

The second he said it, I happened to see a flash of black and tan away up on a ledge above a lot of outcroppings. Circus' hound stopped stock-still in his tracks and looked back down at his master.

Circus fired up at that and barked to Wally. "Don't you *dare* yell like that again! Ichy thought it was *me* ordering *him* to stop. We've got to let him go, let him do what we want him to!"

"I was yelling at *my* dog!" Wally defended himself. His tone of voice was so surly that I knew if things hadn't been like they were, there might have been a fist fight.

Just that second I heard Little Jim let out a yell from away up ahead of us. I was so astonished I almost jumped out of my tracks. I'd supposed he was behind us.

I looked in the direction his high-pitched, cheerful yell had come from and there he was on the dead trunk of a fallen tree—one end of the tree having landed in its fall on the other side of a narrow gulch. "Look what yesterday's storm did!" he cried back and down to us. "It made a bridge for us to go across on!"

Little Jim was right. The great big old ponderosa pine that had stood so many years all alone on the edge of the gulch had blown over. And there, right out in the middle of the tree bridge, was Little Jim himself holding onto one of the upright branches.

In my mind's eye I was seeing Little Jim's acrobatic actions of the past several weeks—"skinning the cat" on the two-by-four of our grape arbor, balancing himself as he walked across the high beam in our haymow, jumping off into the hay, turning a half somersault in the air and landing on his back in the soft hay, learning to do the cartwheel like Circus, our acrobat, who could do it almost as well as the clown at the Sugar Creek county fair.

What, I cringed, *if that little rascal away out there on that tree-trunk bridge across the chasm with the big boulders and jagged rocks below*

should decide all of a sudden he wanted to put on
some kind of a stunt for us to watch?

What if he was imagining himself to be a stunt man with the rest of us boys an imaginary crowd of thousands of cheering people!

Also, as you can maybe guess if you've ever been a boy or ever known anybody who couldn't help it 'cause he was one, another feeling was in my mind right then. It was this: I, Bill Collins, Theodore Collins' only son, would like to climb up to where the tree bridge was and work my way across to the wide ledge on the other side. That ledge was the one place in all the Sugar Creek territory I had never been. There never before had been any way for us to get there except by going a long way around behind Old Man Paddler's cabin, up and up and up, and then letting ourselves down on a rope. We had talked about doing it but had decided it was too dangerous and too dumb for a boy to do.

If Little Jim should lose his balance or accidentally let go the upright branch he was holding onto, what would happen? There wasn't any net for him to fall into like the acrobat at the fair had had, only rocks and . . . .

The thought had to be shut out of my mind— and nobody ought to put it into Little Jim's mind either or he *might* get scared, lose his balance, fall and—and—

I used as calm a voice as I could, called up to him to be careful, to come back across to our side, and to wait till we could come up and examine the bridge to see if it was safe to try to cross on. If only I could get him to come back before he went any farther.

Several of the rest of us called to him too. Alexander the Coppersmith was at the end of his leash, straining and whimpering to get to wherever Ichabod was, somewhere up ahead of us. Just that second Ichabod let out a fresh, long-toned, wailing tremolo. It sounded now as if he had worked his way across the canyon and was on the other side somewhere not far from the place where his mother and her big rangy hunting dog companion had always lost the trail before.

Our voices warning Little Jim to wait for us and to go on across were like Circus' orders to Ichabod for him to stop. They only spurred him on. He called back to us, "Who's afraid of the big bad wolf?"

Wally called up to him then, and said, "It's a wildcat we're after, not a wolf," which was an unnecessary remark, I thought.

Anyway, it didn't help any. Little Jim carefully worked his way across the broad tree-trunk bridge and in a jiffy there he was on the other side on the ledge, waving back to us and calling "Come on up and over! Come on in; the water's fine!" That's nearly always what the first one in the old swimming hole yells back to the rest of us.

There was another voice then. Ichabod Brown's voice all of a sudden broke out into an excited series of bawls, barks, yelps, and chops that said he was getting close to his quarry and for us all to come and help him or else *watch* him make short work of a fierce-fanged wildcat.

Then what to my wondering eyes should appear but a flash of black and tan about a hundred yards from where Little Jim was on the very same long wide ledge. He was working his way around the base of a gnarled, weather-killed, twisted juniper whose roots were somewhere below in the side of the cliff. I cringed as I watched him zigzagging here and there, nose first, sniffing at the face of the cliff to see if Old Stubtail had gone up. He acted like there was so much wildcat smell on the ledge it was as hard for him to find the trail as it would be for a boy to work his way blindfolded through a brier patch. Every second, though, he was getting nearer to Little Jim.

At a narrow place on the ledge where there was another juniper, I saw a bird fly from a nest and go scooting along the ledge for maybe ten or twenty

113

feet before taking wing out across the sky. For only a few seconds, Ichabod stopped, stood pointed-nosed at it, then dropped his head to the rocky ledge he was on as much as to say, *"That,* is trash! My master wants me to stick to my job!" And he was busy again, snuffling his way toward where Little Jim was near the top end of the tree-trunk bridge. Little Jim was proud of himself for not being afraid and was maybe imagining himself to be a clown high in a big outdoor tent doing acrobatic stunts.

And then, like a streak of lightning going through my mind, I saw a flash of grayish-brown animal between Little Jim and Ichabod. He was backed up against the cliff, his ears flattened, ready to fight tooth and talon and fang anything or anybody.

At almost the very same second I saw him, Ichabod changed his tone and was barking "treed." That little untrained, unafraid dog-child of one of the best hunting hounds in the country, Mrs. Bawler Brown, had succeeded where his mother and Old Jay had failed a half-dozen times. He'd trailed a colt-killing, pig-stealing, sheep-killing marauder to its lair.

I say lair 'cause that's where right that second Old Stubtail was—under an overhanging rock

114

where there was a deep depression in the cliff wall going back in maybe four feet.

The only way for the wildcat to get away from Ichabod now would be to come still farther this way—and "this way" was where Little Jim was. Also, I noticed, there as only ten feet more of ledge for Little Jim to retreat to, if he had to. There, just those ten feet from him, was the *end* of the ledge. It stopped at a rock wall that went straight up.

Any second now Ichabod would be close enough for Stubtail to thrust out a long, savage, talon-filled paw, rake that little purebred pup in, and either tear him to pieces or open his jaws and just bite through his head. And that'd be the last of one of the finest little dogs there ever was.

For the first time then Little Jim realized what a danger he was in. He realized it on account of all of us were yelling to him to get to the tree-trunk bridge and come back. The "cat" was closer to the tree trunk than he was. In fact the depression in the wall, was almost at the very end of the treetop.

In a minute now Ichabod would be there. There'd be a savage half-minute fight, and it'd be all over—for Ichabod. And what would happen to Little Jim?

Something had to be done. I knew, and I guess Wally and Circus and Poetry realized the same

115

thing, that not a one of us could get there in time to help Little Jim.

I already had Betty Lizzie loaded and was on my way toward the fallen ponderosa trunk. But how could I shoot when Ichabod was leaping in and out snapping at Old Stubtail? And Little Jim was in my line of fire too!

In my hurry and because of the cyclone in my mind, I quickly stooped, picked up a three-foot-long club from a dead tree, whirled, and threw it as hard as I could straight for the cliff wall near Little Jim. "Use this club to fight with if you have to!" I yelled across to him.

Just that second Ichabod was there, and the fight was on. Circus was screaming for him to stop, but Ichabod didn't realize he was supposed to be only a trailer and not a catch dog. He was in the fight tooth and toenail and so far was being missed by all the wildcat's savage thrusts with his claws.

Little Jim saw the club strike the wall, bounce back, and fall not more than six feet from the fight. He quick stooped and made a dive for it. I guess Old Stubtail thought he was being attacked from two sides, that he had to fight not only a dog but a human being as well.

He whirled from Ichabod and faced Little Jim, his fangs bared, his voice snarling. And in another minute I expected to see Little Jim get killed.

I couldn't stand it to look, but I also couldn't look away.

But something else was going on. A city-bred mongrel of a dog that wasn't afraid of anything except a snapping turtle and that had been trained to chase after every club anybody threw anywhere —with all the excitement going on on the other side of the gully instead of where he was—had come to wild life at the end of Wally's leash. He always wanted to be in the middle of whatever excitement there was. Alex reared, plunged, and pulled savagely. And like a covey of quail being flushed, he was gone, and only a leash with an empty dog collar on it was left in Wally's hand.

A copper-colored streak with four flying legs on it was on its way to the broad tree-trunk bridge, out on it, and across. And with a rush of flying teeth and legs and barks he was headfirst into the middle of a wildcat fight.

He'd chased a dangerous black and white house cat under a barn, and driven a wild cottontail down a hedgerow to Poetry's dad's woods. Now he was on the way to save all of us and Ichabod and Little Jim from an insignificant wildcat that he could lick with one tooth.

Before you could have said Jack Robinson Crusoe, Alexander the Coppersmith was there. He was there head-and-teeth-first and he *didn't* get stopped by flying cat claws. He rushed in, getting there while Little Jim was still standing, club raised ready to strike, to try to stop Old Stubtail's flying tackle as he sprang toward the cutest little guy that was ever a member of the Sugar Creek Gang.

In another second—or even a half second— that'd have been the end of little Jim.

And *then* is when Alexander the Coppersmith struck, his whole body whamming into the wildcat at full weight. There was so much fast and noisy action for a few seconds you couldn't even see what was happening.

Only one thing I knew and that was that Alexander the Coppersmith, city-bred dog that couldn't be managed, wouldn't obey orders, had landed head-and-teeth-first into the center of a new kind of dog game.

It was all over before we realized it had started. The cat and Alexander the Coppersmith, scratching and biting and rolling and hissing, got too near the edge and over they went together—*down . . . down . . . down . . . DOWN!*

I heard their bodies crash on the rocks below and saw them bound off a jutting ledge down there and go hurtling to the bottom of the canyon.

10

It took us quite a while to work our way down the sides of the canyon wall to the bottom where Old Stubtail and Alexander were, and it was hard to believe what we found when we did get there.

Wally, sobbing and holding onto his empty leash, reached the scene first. The rest of us got there only a few seconds later—we having to wait for Little Jim to come back across the broad tree-trunk bridge before we started.

All the way down I kept remembering what had happened on the ledge—the whole exciting, dangerous thing: Stubtail with his back to the declivity in the canyon wall, his ears flattened in anger, his body crouching ready to spring at Ichabod. Then he realized Little Jim was not more than five feet from him with a club in his hand and, maybe deciding in a flash that Little Jim was going to try to kill him, he had made a flying leap straight for that little guy.

What made the whole excitement even more

like a tornado was a copper-colored city dog who didn't know what danger was streaking across the broad tree-trunk bridge and crashing head-on with the wildcat, meeting Old Stubtail in mid-air. And Little Jim's life had been saved.

It was one of the saddest sights we ever saw. It just didn't seem possible, but it was the truth and we had to believe it. Not more than two feet apart on a pile of jagged rocks were the broken and bloody bodies of the tufted-eared, stub-tailed, fierce-fanged colt-killer and a nonsensical, uncontrollable, reckless mongrel. Little Jim, with tears in his eyes, stood with the rest of us in our little semicircle and was the first one to say anything. He broke out into loud crying as he sobbed, "He saved my life! He got there just in time!"

I guess we were all about as sad as we ever were in our lives on account of Alexander the Coppersmith getting killed in the fall on the rocks, but we were glad too that our own Little Jim was alive and with us. For just a second I had a flash of a thought in my mind of a golden stairway leading up and up and up, and it seemed like maybe an angel had come swooping down and *that* was the reason Little Jim had been saved. Anyway, he *was* spared and I knew who had spared him, even if He had used a dog to do it. It felt fine to believe that.

Wally said something then, bringing my thoughts back to our sad circle. I guess I had forgotten that the last time he had come to visit us we had made him a member of the gang and that he had decided to become a Christian, too. But when he said what he said right then, the *way* he said it, so reverently and with tears in his voice—and also while he was on his knees trying to hug his dead dog—I all of a sudden went blind with my own tears. I never will forget what he said, as long as I live:

"Old pal, I guess God had a plan for *your* life, too!" Then he broke into hysterical sobbing like people sometimes do at a funeral.

I didn't get a chance to use Betty Lizzie on Old Stubtail because he was already dead. One thing we all noticed was that there was a jagged, bloody place in his throat, as if some animal of some kind had sunk its teeth into him. We knew *what* animal had done it when, a few seconds later, we noticed Wally picking little tufts of wildcat fur from Alexander's teeth.

At first we thought we'd try to get Alexander's body home and, as Little Jim suggested right then, "bury him under the papaw bushes and put up a tombstone, and every year on Memorial Day, put flowers there and—"

But Wally said, cutting in on him, "No, we'll

121

bury him right here. Right where he fell in battle."

Wally had a right to decide it since he was the nearest relative. Besides, when I looked up the steep canyon wall and thought about the long trip through the swamp and how heavy Alexander was, I knew the pallbearers would have a very hard time of it.

I took off my hat in a hurry and used it to shoo away several bluebottle flies that had come from somewhere and were buzzing about the two corpses at our feet—which was another reason why we ought to have the funeral right away.

"How come you want to bury him *here*?" Dragonfly wanted to know. Wally answered, "Don't they have a cemetery at Gettysburg where the Battle of Gettysburg was fought?"

Poetry, being good in history, said they did. "They dedicated it on November 19, 1863. That's when Abraham Lincoln made his famous Gettysburg address."

First we dragged Old Stubtail back fifteen or twenty feet then, with our bare hands and with sticks and sharp rocks, scooped out a place for Alexander's grave.

So it wouldn't be too shallow a grave, on account of it was pretty hard and rocky soil to dig in, we piled rocks and rocks and more rocks on top.

We stepped back to look at it—not a one of us

saying anything but all of us fighting tears and most of us gulping a little. Then we faced east like people do on Armistice Day in respect for the dead, took off all our hats, and stood with our heads bowed a minute or two. And the funeral was over.

The wildcat was even heavier than Alexander, but we decided to try to take him home. Getting him to the top of the canyon wall was the hardest. Ichabod was acting very happy, but the gang wasn't. Ordinarily we'd have felt proud of ourselves, Circus especially 'cause it was his own cute little black and tan dog that had done a better job of trailing than his experienced mother—better, even, than Old Jay, one of the best-known "cat" catchers in the whole country.

When we reached the place where the ponderosa had fallen, Circus stopped us all and surprised us with, "You guys stay here a minute, I want to go across and see if I can find her cubs!"

"HER cubs!" different ones of us exploded back at him.

"Yes," Circus answered grimly. "HER Cubs. Old Stubtail was a mother!"

And Circus was right. Stubtail *was* a mother. Her body showed she'd been nursing her babies, maybe that very day.

Wally spoke up then and said, 'I want one of them for a pet."

I remembered how last year he'd wanted a pet polecat and had actually taken a descented one home with him to Memory City.

But I'll have to stop writing now—in just a few minutes, anyway—on account of the adventure we had later coming back and taking two cute little kitten wildcats alive is another story which, added onto this one, would make it too long.

For some reason, though, when I found out about there being two little wildcat babies left motherless and thought how their mother—who was what is called "carnivorous" and *had* to have raw flesh to eat because that was the way she was made—well it was hard to be glad she was dead.

I *could* be glad, though, that she wouldn't steal any more of Old Red Addie's cute little curly-tailed pigs nor any of Harm Groenwald's lambs nor anybody's baby colts, and I was thankful that Little Jim's life had been saved.

Poetry, my best friend, explained it to Wally and me a little later that day when Dad and I were over at his house waiting for dinner to be ready. We were in his tent in their backyard at the time, the same tent we'd had such a topsy-turvy adventure in in the story, *10,000 Minutes at Sugar Creek*.

He was showing us his shell collection at the

time. "See all these empty shells?" he asked Wally and me.

"They certainly are pretty," Wally answered. He had one of Poetry's dull-white, two-and-a-half-inch-long Iceland cockles in his hand admiring it, and I could see maybe he'd want to start a hobby of collecting shells himself some time.

Poetry had something special on his mind, I could tell from the way he was wrinkling his forehead. I knew for sure when he said, "Once there was a bivalve mollusk living in this little shell house. But it died and left its shell behind. Everything in nature has to die some time."

I heard Wally gulp. I knew he was thinking about a pile of stones up in Old Man Paddler's rocky hills where, at the bottom of a ravine, Alexander the Coppersmith lay buried.

It wasn't pleasant to think what we were all thinking right then, but we couldn't help it. I was glad, though, that we were interrupted a few jiffies later by a high-pitched tremolo from the direction of the backdoor. It was Poetry's mother wanting us to come to dinner.

It had been an exciting day. My mind had certainly had a lot of things to think about. That night when I was upstairs in my room getting ready to go to bed, I stood for a few minutes looking out at the moonlit back yard, past the chicken house and Addie's apartment. It seemed I was a whole lot older than I had been this time last night—years and years and years. So much had happened.

I had learned a lot of different things. Wally was in the other room in his own bed, sound alseep. I could tell by the snoring, which I remembered from last year.

Then, like my parents had taught me to, I knelt beside my bed to make a sort of good-night prayer to the heavenly Father and to ask Him for anything that might be on my mind.

I was surprised when I heard myself whispering to Him, "Please help Bill Collins not to be a trash-trailer in life. . . . Help me to find out for sure what You want me to be and to stay on the track without getting off on anything You *don't* want me to. . . . Help me to do only what is right. . . ."

I can't remember finishing my prayer nor getting into bed. But I *must* have finished it, and I *must* have crawled in between Mom's nice clean sheets because only a few jiffies later (or so it seemed). I was wide-awake in bed, the sun was shining outside, and I could hear birds singing in the woods across the road.